HAVING THE WEREWOLF'S BABY

CHAOTIC CONCEPTIONS
BOOK TWO

COURTNEY DAVIS

5 PRINCE PUBLISHING
5PRINCEBOOKS.COM

Published by:

5 Prince Publishing and Books, LLC

DBA 5 Prince Publishing

PO Box 865

Arvada, Colorado 80001

Digital ISBN: 978-1-63112-430-3

Print ISBN: 978-1-63112-431-0

Cover design by Marianne Nowicki

Interior design by 5 Prince Publishing

First Edition

F12222025

For more information about this title, visit: www.5princebooks.com

To my husband,
you have been the biggest support in my writing,
and I can't tell you how much that has helped me to continue.

ACKNOWLEDGMENTS

Thank you to Bernadette for continuing to release my work,
your ongoing belief in my writing is priceless.

Cate, thank you for all the work you do to help me edit my
writing,
it wouldn't be such a great final product without your input and
skill.
Also, your comments make me smile knowing at least one person
gets me!

ALSO BY COURTNEY DAVIS

Chaotic Conception Series

Having the Vampire's Baby

Having the Werewolf's Baby

The Atlantis Series

The Vampires of Atlantis

Aristotle's Wolves

Descendants of Atlantis

Stand Alone Titles

Butterfly Kisses

The Serpent and the Firefly

A Spider in the Garden

Princess of Prias

Soul Sacrifice

A Shadow Among the Stars

Demons and Tea Leaves

Trusting the Alpha

HAVING THE WEREWOLF'S BABY

PROLOGUE: TWENTY YEARS AGO

Onyx stood outside the Stonecroft Fertility Clinic and growled. He just wanted to put as much distance as possible between himself and his father, but that took cash. This was the quickest way he could figure out to get enough money for him to make it to his new home. The home he'd bought with every last cent in his bank account instead of paying for his junior year of college.

"Welcome to the Stonecroft Clinic," a cheerful witch behind the front counter called out as he slunk inside the sterile feeling waiting room. He felt out of place in his worn jeans, old boots, and ripped flannel shirt, but the front desk attendant didn't even blink at his appearance. "How can I help you today?" she asked when he approached the desk.

He ran a hand through his hair, it was cut short the way his father liked. He thought he might never cut it again because he answered to no one but himself anymore. "I guess I'm looking to make a little quick cash," he whispered, eyes downcast. If anyone ever found out about this, he'd be mortified. Ironically, he was running away from a pregnancy and yet here he was offering up his sperm for some unknown couple in need.

"Semen for artificial insemination then," she said with a smile and pulled out a clipboard. "Fill this out and take a seat, someone will call you back to a room soon."

He took the clipboard and dropped into a seat wondering if he should make up the information he was putting down. How would anyone know?

"You'll have to show ID," the witch behind the desk called out as if she'd read his mind and he didn't hold back a growl.

The witch just rolled her eyes.

He decided there was no harm in the truth anyway, this was a confidential agreement. He scanned the paperwork briefly, it seemed like what he'd expected and he didn't really care what they did with his sperm once he had the necessary money in his hand.

A smile threatened to lift his lips when he wrote his address, his new address, his freedom. It was a little slice of heaven all his own and it was far outside of Oceanview and past the city of Larkspring. It was even a few miles outside of the small town of Greensferry which was nestled at the base of the Southern California foothills. He couldn't wait to settle in there and maybe never talk to anyone ever again.

He may be alone for the rest of his life, but at least he wouldn't be forced into marriage and a life that would fit him like a straitjacket.

He handed the witch his paperwork then sat back down and picked up a magazine. The cover showed the clinic and the two witch sisters, Felicity and Gina Stonecroft, who had opened it just last year. The headline praised the clinic for the number of pregnancies it had assisted in already, and not just human pregnancies, it was making a real difference for vampires who tended to have trouble with fertility. Onyx assumed it was the fact that it was the first clinic to be run by witches that was the key to its success.

"Mr. West," a nurse called a few minutes later. She had his completed form in her hands and a bright smile that really didn't sit well with him seeing as he was about to go jerk off into a cup for money. "Right this way, we are very excited to have your semen. We don't get a lot of werewolves in here, so I'm sure your sample will be snatched up by a werewolf couple struggling with infertility quickly." When he didn't make a response she added, "You're doing a really great thing."

Onyx just snorted. He didn't care about helping anyone but himself. He followed the woman back to a room with a bench seat and low lighting. There was a stack of magazines, a basket full of what he assumed were various lubes, and a sink to wash his hands in when he was done. He'd never felt less like jerking off since he'd learned he could.

"Here you go, is there anything particular you require? Like I said, we don't get a lot of werewolves in here." She spoke in a soft but professional tone that he appreciated, there was no reason to make this situation more awkward.

Onyx shook his head and entered the room, taking the sticker from her that he was supposed to attach to the cup when he was done. It was nothing but a number that would match the number at the top of the form he'd filled out. It was meant to keep him anonymous, which was good, he didn't ever want to know what happened from here. He did like the idea of his semen—such a scientific term for what happened between him and his hand in here—going to a couple that would truly love and appreciate the gift of a child.

An hour later Onyx's truck was gassed up and he was heading out of town. He was two hours from his new home and his new solitary existence. He couldn't wait to live out the rest of his life the way he wanted. He didn't need anyone, didn't want anyone, and no one out there would be trying to control him.

CHAPTER ONE

Twenty years later...

Felicity Stonecroft stood in her yard under the full moon and threw herbs into the fire. It had been a year since she was given a task by the Moon Goddess that resulted in delightful chaos, and a baby, for a human and vampire. Tonight she welcomed the answer of any spirit willing to talk to her, but she had her favorite. She'd woken in the middle of the night, a usual occurrence on nights when the moon was full and bright, and walked out here to begin the ritual. She was a willing conduit to the gods and goddesses who wanted to insert themselves into the lives of those in Oceanview. She wasn't surprised when the Moon Goddess appeared in the flames before her, She'd become a familiar entity in Felicity's life.

"And what kind of chaos are you hoping for now?" Felicity cackled as she was surrounded by the cold presence of the goddess.

A face and a number appeared in Felicity's mind.

"I am but a servant to your chaotic will," she said with a slick smile spreading across her face. She'd been waiting for this one. The moment the semen had come into the clinic she'd known it was special because it had pulsed with the promise of the goddess. She'd saved it twenty years for this.

≈

When Aurora Port had moved into the small cottage she'd inherited from her grandmother, she'd known all about the grumpy werewolf neighbor. He was the only neighbor within a five-mile radius and their two modest homes sat together at the end of a dirt road separated by their unfenced yards. Aurora knew her grandmother hadn't believed in fencing nature out or in, but she wasn't sure what had kept the werewolf from walling himself off from everyone and everything.

According to Aurora's grandmother, Beatrice Port, her neighbor didn't talk to or interact with anyone in town, but he didn't cause trouble either. He was basically your run-of-the-mill reclusive grump, no different than any other mountain man tucked away in the California hills. The only thing that had always struck Aurora as odd about him before they'd met was that he was a werewolf and it was rare to find a werewolf who isolated himself as much as he seemed to.

He hadn't ever been a bother to her grandmother though, so Aurora didn't worry about living next to him herself even if she'd be alone without any neighbors within screaming distance. Beatrice had actually spoken well of the man. She'd said he was a good neighbor; *a nice man, but quiet.* Aurora thought maybe her grandmother was just too senile to realize the man was weirdly antisocial. Especially since in all the times Aurora had visited her grandmother before her death, Aurora hadn't once seen the man.

So when Aurora moved into the inherited house she'd expected the neighbor to be eighty with only a few teeth, wafting body odor, and clothes in need of washing and mending. Seeing a mid-thirties hot-bodied man with dark brown hair pulled up in a messy knot atop his head and wild brown eyes stalking across the neighbor's yard, she'd assumed this was a grandson. He was tan and shirtless, in a pair of cutoff shorts and bare feet with a few days of unshaved scruff darkening his strong chin. Obviously he was fresh from some kind of manly work judging by the sheen of sweat glistening on his skin. It was like one of her most erotic dreams come to life.

Her body had reacted immediately to the sight. Her nipples became sensitive nubs and her heart started to race with desire. She had even squeezed her thighs together as if in anticipation of having him shoved between them. His face or his cock, she wasn't picky. He was her brand of male company and she wasn't the type of woman to act coy about it.

She shook herself out of her desire spiral and remembered her manners. She had been raised mostly by her hippie mother who had instilled kindness and community into her DNA. So of course, without hesitation she had hurried over in her yellow sundress and sandals. She planned to greet him and hopefully get his number. Maybe he'd inherit his grandfather's property someday and they'd be neighbors. Neighbors who shared hot sweaty sexy time.

"Who the fuck are you and why are you on my property?" he'd growled at her before she'd even opened her mouth.

Aurora had stiffened and pulled up all the fight she'd learned from her dad who wasn't a hippie like her mom. He was a cop in Larkspring, and he didn't take shit from anyone.

"I am the new neighbor, is that how you greet everyone?" She'd snapped back with a saccharine sweetness that anyone over the age of ten would have read perfectly.

He narrowed his eyes at her. "Yes, now get off my lawn," he'd snarled back at her.

"Your lawn?"

"Mine."

This wasn't the grandson she realized, this was the cranky recluse. She'd flipped him off, he'd glared harder, and then she'd sauntered back to her property without any rush. It was really too bad he was every bit the asshole the people in town had said he was because he was also a wet dream.

That moment set the tone for how their relationship had gone on for the past three years. She'd learned his full name by snooping in his mail, which he had caught her doing and looked like he wanted to bite her hand off for. She'd merely said "Oops, sorry Onyx." And walked away feeling his glare as she went. It hadn't taken long to realize he was all bark and no bite. No one in town had proof that he was dangerous or violent, they just said he was grumpy and mean and because he was a werewolf, they took that as scary. Rumor in town was that he was about forty as best they could assume by how long he'd been living there. He'd maintained a very young physique due to an active lifestyle and being a werewolf.

Onyx had repaid the intrusion on his mail by pissing on her daffodils and they hadn't grown that first spring. She'd repaid that by *accidentally* throwing wolfsbane seeds in his front lawn causing him to have to dig up the grass and replant it.

Their hate-hate relationship had become a comfortable space to live in. She sprinkled wolfsbane seeds heavily along their property line, and on full moon nights she heard him howling in the woods behind her house. If she sometimes thought about those precious moments before he'd opened his mouth that first day while she was pleasuring herself, well, that was unavoidable and harmless.

CHAPTER TWO

Tonight was a full moon and Aurora fully expected to hear Onyx's howls soon, not that it bothered her. She'd stopped being unnerved by it after the first couple of months. He howled, never very close, and that was it, no big deal. She did try to stay inside on these nights despite the fact that she knew werewolves didn't become feral beasts on the full moon. There was no reason to tempt fate and end up werewolf chow because honestly, it was hard to tell how deep Onyx's hatred of her went.

"Are you sure this is what you want to do Aurora B?" Her mother, Bea Port, asked wistfully over the phone. She knew her mother was really feeling her spiritual self when she called her by her full name. The B stood for two things, Borealis and Beatrice. She was named after the lights her mother had seen in the sky the night she'd been conceived. It was a story that no child should know about their parents, but her mother had always been too much of a free spirit not to share. The name also carried on the tradition of naming daughters after themselves. Her grandmother had been Beatrice, named her daughter Bea, and Aurora got B as a middle name. She wasn't sure what she'd do for her own daughter if she had one, can't really shorten a letter.

"I'm sure."

"Have you tried laying out in fresh turned soil under the full moon then collecting your next cycle's blood and burying it under some lavender? That's how I got your father to come to me. We had such a wonderful month after that and then I had you."

Aurora rolled her eyes at the familiar tale. Her parents had never really been together but had gotten pregnant after a few dates and co-parented her rather well despite their very opposite lifestyles.

"I haven't tried that, no, but I have taken a look at everyone in town and firmly decided they shouldn't be the father of my child." Which is why she was sitting on her couch looking through a binder of artificial insemination candidates. Admittedly not the typical activity for someone her age. It's not as if menopause was looming. She just knew what she wanted and she wasn't afraid to go get it. That was something she'd learned from both her parents.

"And you need a child, now?" Bea asked carefully, never one to try and over-parent. "You could always take a summer trip and meet someone."

"The Moon Goddess sent me a message. It is time for me to have a baby, no more waiting. Besides, I'm halfway through my thirties, how much longer do you think I should wait? I think it's better to do it on my own anyway versus sharing the experience with a one-night stand or a short-term boyfriend." She hoped that statement wouldn't offend her mother.

"This is because Trent broke up with you, isn't it?" She asked, no offense taken to the slight against Bea's own path to parenthood.

"He didn't break up with me, he cheated on me. With one of the other teachers in my building and got her pregnant while we were still dating," Aurora seethed. It was the latest in a long line of bad relationships and she was so over dating. "I broke up with him when I found out." And she then had to keep working with Carol who teaches art at the high school where Aurora taught science. She kept her professionalism at the forefront though, because she wasn't going to lose her job too over Trent and Carol's betrayal. It wasn't easy in a small town to keep something like that a secret though and her students quickly heard the rumors. She guiltily felt good about the fact that they all seemed to be on her side and started to give Carol the cold shoulder. Thankfully, it was almost summer break now and the cheaters were moving to San Francisco to be closer to Carol's family.

"Okay love, you know I'll support you in anything and I can't wait to be a grandmother."

Aurora let out a sigh. "I know, thanks Mom." The sound of howling drew Aurora's attention to the kitchen window. "Why the hell is he so close this month?" she grumbled. She could usually tell he was on the outskirts of her back property, but this sounded like he was standing in her garden which was just a few feet from her back porch.

"Oh, that handsome feral neighbor of yours?" her mother asked slyly. "Why not see if he's interested in a little bed play? I'd bet he has potent sperm."

"Werewolf sperm, I don't think humans and werewolves can produce children, so I'll pass." Not to mention actually having that angry man pumping away above her was more the stuff of nightmares than fantasy. He'd probably frown down at her and tell her all the ways she was doing it wrong. He loved to correct her and wasn't quiet about the fact he hated the way she let the crabgrass grow, hated the way she spread wildflower seeds, hated the way she left her door open on hot evenings.

She did fantasize about him more than she'd like to admit but the reality of him was a hard pass.

"Your loss. You know I dated a few werewolves in my time; great fun, and so passionate."

"I'll take that under advisement," Aurora said sarcastically.

7

"Talk to you tomorrow," she assured her mom and hung up. She went back to perusing the list of possible donors until she found one that sounded good. He described himself as an athletic male with dark hair and eyes, the opposite of her. She was active, but not athletic by any means and she had blue-green eyes like her father and light blonde hair that matched her mother's. She liked the idea of mixing with her opposite, it would give her child a well-rounded set of DNA. The bio also said he enjoyed landscaping and bicycling, and that he had a college degree, education was important to her. "Well hello number 439, you just might get lucky next week."

Aurora had been preparing for the insemination for a while now, though she hadn't told her mother how far she'd already gone toward the procedure. She was currently shot full of hormones and had an appointment the following week to be inseminated. This was the last step, picking the sperm. She sent off an email to the clinic with her choice of donor and a thrill trickled down her spine.

She wandered into her little kitchen to pour a celebratory glass of wine. She was finishing the last bottle in the house since she'd be abstaining for a while. Not that she was much of a drinker anyway, but she usually had a glass or two on the weekends, teaching was stressful. She sipped the crisp white and looked out the kitchen window when she heard another howl that was all too close. A shadow streaked through her backyard making her frown. Why the hell was he pushing so close tonight? Her lips twisted up in an evil grin and she went to the sprinkler controls on the back porch.

A couple of buttons later she heard the sprinkler system kick on. "Get off my lawn," she yelled.

Aurora went back to her couch with her wine and sent a text off to her best friend. Claire was a math teacher at the high school and they'd shared a wall for years. Claire was perky, lively, and fun, which was everything Aurora enjoyed in who she spent her time with. Claire was also extremely supportive, so Aurora wasn't surprised when she messaged back with a picture of two girls jumping up and down in celebration followed by a cute baby wearing a birthday hat.

Aurora put her feet up on her coffee table and grabbed her popcorn, feeling content in the life she was creating for herself. She hit play on one of her favorite romantic comedies and settled in to enjoy the rest of her night.

Onyx snarled and ran from the spray of water. He knew he was too close to Aurora's house, but his wolf instincts were harder to ignore in this form and she smelled far more fertile than normal. It was messing with him. Usually he was satisfied with staying at the edges of her property, pissing around the place to keep out predators and any horny werewolves that might slink into the area not realizing it was claimed already. This was his territory and by extension, she was his. Not in a mate kind of way, just in a way that he didn't want his neighbor meeting and inviting another werewolf around.

The lead up to this full moon had been different, he'd been more anxious and irritable but couldn't pinpoint why. The usual excitement to stretch out in his other form had been missing and when he did shift he had been assaulted by the smell of her. She was fertile. She shouldn't be *that* fertile at this time of the month, or ever. It was distracting to the point that he was unable to take his usual route around the outskirts of both their properties. His instincts demanded that he stay close and protect her from all other males while she was in such a vulnerable state.

Honestly, it was telling him to do a hell of a lot more than that, but even his wolf instincts couldn't get him to ignore the fact that she was the most infuriating woman he'd ever met in his life. No amount of full moon amorous energy or scent of fertility could make him forget that.

Shaking off in his own yard, he sat and howled up at the moon. He knew her cycle like his own and he didn't understand what was going on. It was as if she'd increased her hormonal output tenfold somehow.

It wasn't that he *liked* knowing, or that he tracked it because he cared. No, he tracked it because when she was at her most fertile and he caught her scent, his cock hardened. And liking her, even just physically, made him want to scratch his own eyes out. She was annoying on a good day, which brought a new thought into his mind. Was this some new way she'd found to make his life miserable?

Anger burned through his veins. Did she have any idea what kind of dangerous game she was playing by flaunting her hormones under a wolf's nose? If he was a different type of man, he'd be a danger to her in this scenario, but he wasn't. He had never been the kind of man to take a violent hand or even an entitled approach to women. He liked mutual respect and understanding, he liked what a woman could offer him and what he could do for her in return. But he knew not all men were like that and it kept him close to her when he'd rather be far enough away that he couldn't detect her scent.

Of course she probably had no idea or care about what her hormone spike could do to him. She thought she was above reproach, and everyone in town agreed. They all thought Aurora Port shit sunshine, but he knew she was vindictive and conniving, and she made him miserable. She'd invaded his peace three years ago and he hadn't been completely relaxed since.

Living next to Aurora's grandmother, Beatrice, had been easy and quiet. The old woman kept to herself, other than baking him cookies occasionally. He'd returned the favor by keeping an eye on her from afar and every once in a while he mowed her lawn.

Aurora had immediately been aggressively friendly. She had rushed onto his property in a bright fucking sundress with her ridiculously long—so blonde it was almost white—hair flying loosely around her. When she'd gotten close he was momentarily dumbstruck by the brightness of her green eyes as they bored into him with curiosity. Her wide full lips were cherry red and there was a spray of freckles across her slightly upturned nose that annoyed him for reasons he wasn't willing to investigate.

He hated her intrusion then, and he hated it even more now because it wasn't her friendship and neighborly greetings she was shoving at him. No, this was so much worse. She was shoving her fertility up his nostrils like a goddamn seductress, or a succubus, trying to lure him into her trap. It wouldn't work though. His hatred for the little bit of sunshine was far too great to be overridden by sexual or reproductive instinct.

Unable to go completely against those impulses in this form, however, he paced along their property line for the next couple of hours. Forgoing the usual hunt for small animals in order to just watch her house. Sometime after midnight he laid down in the grass and fell asleep.

Onyx woke up as the rising sun licked at his naked skin and trudged back to his house, resenting everything about his neighbor even more than usual. She'd managed to ruin one more thing in his life.

Usually he woke from a full moon run with a full belly and a satisfied wolf. This morning felt like he'd been on an all night bender.

He showered then collapsed on his mattress. His cat, Peggy, jumped up to cuddle with him and purred soothingly.

"Why do you like me? I would eat you if I let you outside on the full moon." He told her the same thing every month.

She just blinked her green eyes at him and continued to purr. Somehow this animal had no sense of self-preservation, and he loved her for it. The little white fluffball had shown up on his porch when Aurora had moved in next door. He'd thought maybe it was hers, but it wasn't. He knew that because she'd never complained about a missing cat, not because he'd asked her. He'd let the thing inside his house on accident and when it had curled up in his lap he was lost to its baseless trust of him. Now he had no intention of ever letting her go, which is why she was strictly an inside cat no matter what she might have been before she came to him.

He liked to think it was a gift from the universe. A small piece of friendship and family. The only one he ever expected to get and the only one he wanted.

CHAPTER THREE

Aurora was full of excitement when she drove to the clinic in Oceanview, a little nervous too, but mostly excited. The school year had just ended and she was ready to spend her summer preparing for this life-changing step and deciding what exactly she'd tell people when they asked who the father was. Then when she admitted there was no father, planning her response to *why would you try and do this alone?* She knew that she was a strong, independent woman, exactly like her parents had raised her to be, and she would raise a child the same way all on her own. It helped that she had the promise of the Moon Goddess making her confident that this was the right decision. This was exactly what her life path was supposed to look like, she was certain.

She'd chosen the Stonecroft Clinic despite the two-hour drive, because it was well known in the area. Even nationally known ever since the vampire congressman, Johnson Paulie, announced that his son had a human inseminated there. It'd been all over the news not only because it was a high-profile person, but because it was a human and vampire mix. Interspecies dating, and marrying even, wasn't too rare but having children together was almost unheard of. Aurora liked that the various species were coexisting so well. She'd heard about how hard things had been about fifty years ago when they all started to step out of the dark. Now there was an acceptance that was just beginning to turn into true integration.

She chuckled as she thought Onyx probably would have preferred things the way they'd been before. He didn't strike her as the inclusive type.

Aurora walked into the clinic with head high and full of hope. This was it, and she didn't even have to fake an orgasm, she didn't have to pretend to like war movies, and she didn't have to lie about how much attention she really wanted from a partner. She was getting exactly what she asked for without a guilt trip or tit-for-tat negotiation. She checked in at the front desk then sat on the edge of her seat, too excited to read any of the magazines set out in the waiting room.

"Ms. Port," a nurse called.

Heart pounding, Aurora stood and almost forgot her purse in her rush to go with the woman. "That's me," she said brightly.

The nurse gave her a wide smile. "Welcome to the Stonecroft Clinic. You're here for insemination today, is that right?"

"That's right, I emailed Felicity Stonecroft with my choice."

"Wonderful," the nurse beamed. "Follow me."

Aurora was led back to a little room where she was weighed and then after her vitals were taken, was left alone to strip halfway. She waited on the table with a paper blanket covering her naked lower half and she had no regrets or second thoughts. But she did have the weird sense of unfairness when she thought about how the men who came in to donate the sperm were given porn and a low-lit room where they orgasmed and all she got was a bright light focused on her nether regions and a speculum. At least there was a meadow scene painted on the ceiling for her to stare at while she lay there. It was far better than the dirty ceiling fans of past boyfriends' bedrooms, or that one guy who had a life size poster of a sea turtle advertising something about them choking on plastic in the ocean. It was pretty hard to reach orgasm when you were wondering if you were doing enough to keep the oceans clean.

A soft knock told her it was time and Felicity Stonecroft walked in followed by the nurse carrying a tray, undoubtedly holding the sperm. She had a weird urge to greet the goo and offer to buy it a drink. The thought had her laughing in her head and her smile widening.

"You look excited," Felicity said cheerily.

"I am," Aurora assured her and laid back. She put her feet in the stirrups and visualized the success of this procedure. "I am ready for this."

"Well, I am sure this is going to be a particularly lucky insemination," Felicity said with a wink. "I think the Moon Goddess is going to bless this child."

"Me too," Aurora agreed and relaxed. Felicity's reassurance was comforting because she did not have the money to try again if this failed. She was putting her entire nest egg all in this one basket.

"Take a deep breath, this will be all done shortly," Felicity said as she inserted the speculum.

As expected, the procedure wasn't comfortable, but it wasn't terrible either, and it *was* surprisingly quick.

"I'm trying really hard not to make a joke right now about letting you come inside me without buying me dinner first," Aurora said as she took Felicity's hand to help her sit up on the table.

Felicity cackled, "It wouldn't be the first time, and I'm glad to do it. I think this is my favorite part of the job. I am all about women being empowered to have control over when and how they get pregnant. Now, take it easy for the rest of the day and test when your period would normally show up. If you have any pain, nausea, or bleeding, call me right away. When you have that positive test, make an appointment with your chosen OB-GYN."

"I will, thank you."

Felicity and her nurse left Aurora alone to dress. She didn't want to move at first, hoping that if she waited a few more minutes it would be more likely that the sperm would keep heading in the right direction. She knew that it was a ridiculous thought because it had been injected past her cervix, it wouldn't have that far to go. With a whispered prayer to whatever goddess might be listening, she sat up slowly, wincing at the feel of wetness between her thighs.

"It's just the lube for the speculum," she reminded herself. She hadn't just squished out the potential for a baby.

Aurora left the clinic feeling hopeful and full of new life. When she got home she was still feeling high on endorphins so when she saw that her asshole neighbor wasn't home, which was a rare occurrence, she couldn't resist the opportunity. Onyx worked out of his garage, building some admittedly beautiful wood furniture that he sold online. So about twice a month he made a trip to town to ship stuff off and do his grocery shopping. It was the perfect opportunity for messing with him.

Today was no different, despite the fact that she was maybe going to be a mother and so should probably act like a mature adult. She figured she could hold off on making that change until she was sure the procedure had worked. Aurora went over to Onyx's front porch and took the potted plant he had there. She whistled to herself as she carried it across their yards and into her house, then set it in the front window as a sort of trophy. She wasn't trying to keep the little pot of lavender-colored flowers forever, she just wanted to annoy him. She also wanted to get him back because last week when she'd put some laundry outside to dry in the sun she'd brought in at least one less throw blanket than she'd hung up, she was positive. If he wanted the plant, he'd need to give her back the stolen blanket, it was only fair.

Aurora settled on her couch feeling good about her thievery, which was really more of a hostage situation, and rested her body in hopes that one of the inserted sperm would find its way safely to an egg. She snacked on popcorn and turned on the television to an old familiar vampire movie, it was something that would keep her mind off the possibilities swimming around in her body right then. She knew stressing about it would not help anything, and if she could completely forget about it for the next few weeks, that would be ideal. That was unlikely though, she could hardly think of anything else.

That's where she still was an hour later when she heard Onyx's truck rumble down the road. She turned down the volume on the television and listened as his truck door closed. Moments later she heard his front door slam and she smiled. He had noticed, and he was pissed.

CHAPTER FOUR

Onyx was annoyed. The horrible woman had stolen his plant. What the hell was wrong with her? Who stole a plant off of someone's front porch?

The neighbor from hell, that's who. He glared out his kitchen window which faced the side of Aurora's house and tried to decide if he should stalk over there immediately and growl until she gave it back, or if he should wait and steal it back when she left her house. She may not be going to work every day, since it was summer, but he knew she'd still head into town regularly. Because unlike him, she hadn't moved out here to avoid as much social interaction as possible.

Unfortunately, Aurora didn't leave her house over the next week and Onyx almost started to wonder if she was okay, but then he remembered that she stole his plant and he didn't care anymore. He wanted her to leave so he could take it back and if her guilt had made her ill, well then, that was deserved. He had one daydream about her being allergic to the very plant she'd stolen and although it had made him extremely happy to think of the irony, he had been relieved when he saw her walk to the mailbox later that day. She hadn't died of anaphylactic shock, she didn't have a visible rash, and she wasn't coughing. She was dressed for staying home it seemed, just a pair of stretchy shorts and a loose tank top, she wasn't even wearing shoes. Her hair was piled on top of her head in some kind of knot and she lifted her face to the sun after grabbing her mail, as if she were a sunflower seeking energy. He caught himself wondering if she'd develop more freckles throughout the summer, but quickly thrust those thoughts aside and went back to work on the bookcase he was building.

When he finally saw her head to her car a week later wearing a pale purple sundress and sandals, he knew she'd be heading to town. She pulled out of her driveway and he nearly smiled as he pretended to be preoccupied by the piece of wood he was sanding down in front of his garage.

As soon as she was around the corner of the road, he abandoned his project and strode to her house. There was no reason to hurry, she wouldn't be back any time soon. Everything she could have possibly decided to leave the house for was at least a fifteen minute drive.

He used the key from underneath her doormat, it was the same place her grandmother had kept the spare. When the door swung open he was hit by a wall of her scent. Lavender and a feminine musk that would appeal to him if he wasn't aware of how annoying she was. He kept his breathing shallow as he stepped inside but it didn't stop him from taking it all in anyway. There was something different that he was picking up on, a sharp scent that prickled the back of his mind where his wolf senses resided. If he hadn't been watching her house so closely he would have assumed she'd had a visitor recently and that he was picking up on them. But there'd been no one in here except her all that time.

Maybe she *had* been sick after all and it had done something to her chemistry. He shook himself, not wanting to care one way or the other and went to the plant in her front window. He was slightly annoyed to note that it had some fresh growth, she'd taken good care of it.

He turned around, plant in hand, and glanced around the room. It wasn't enough to take back what was his, he needed to take something of hers as well, payback. He had never been inside her house before, not even when her grandmother had been alive. He'd only ever caught glimpses through her windows from afar and never on purpose because he didn't care what kind of space she made for herself. It wasn't as if he were concerned with her nesting abilities as a potential mate. The living room was decorated in bright colors, the opposite of his own style and no surprise to him at all. It was the same way she dressed herself, bright and sunshiny. Her couch was a buttery yellow with coral throw pillows and a lavender blanket tossed across one arm. She had a cheap and well-worn coffee table made from light wood in front of the couch and he frowned at it. It was a piece of shit, and he had an urge to burn the damn thing. He knew he could make a better table in his sleep. His lips curled as he walked over to the offending piece of furniture. A quick inspection of the rest of the room showed it wasn't a set. In fact there were no matching pieces anywhere in the room. It was just a hodgepodge of side tables and bookshelves all made of different woods with different styles and colors. Some she'd taken a paintbrush to, which was likely an improvement over what they'd been when she picked them up. Impulsively, he swept the small table clean of magazines, coasters, and a remote control. Then he picked it up with one arm and walked out of the house.

"Hey, you fucking psycho," Aurora yelled as she crossed his yard a couple hours later.

Onyx straightened from his project, wiping his hands off on his jeans, not that it did much good, he was covered in sawdust as usual. He waited for her to finish stomping over to him with his arms crossed over his bare chest. He didn't miss her eyes flicking down to the pawprint tattoos that went across his pecs and pausing there for a moment before her gaze went even further, hitting his stomach before snapping back up to meet his with a bright appreciation he'd seen in many women's eyes. She was tall for a woman, almost as tall as him but she was what most people would describe as willowy. There wasn't enough to hold onto in his opinion. He liked women with soft and ample curves. He also preferred women who didn't do everything in their power to annoy him.

"Ms. Port, what can I do for you?"

"Cut the shit, where's my table?" Her green eyes flashed with fury and she tossed her long blonde hair over her shoulder. It was loose today and caught the sunlight as it flew behind her, a contrast to the hard set to her face.

Her anger made him happy. He pointed to a pile of scrap, not allowing any expression on his features.

"What the hell is wrong with you? All I did was take care of your plant for a week because you stole one of my blankets. Stealing and vandalizing my property was unnecessary and illegal."

"You trespassed," he growled, ignoring her blanket comment. He *had* taken it. Well technically his wolf had taken it but he didn't think she'd notice, she'd had a few hung up to dry that day.

"You trespass on my property once a month," she snapped back.

Also true, so he ignored it. "That was a piece of junk, it offended me."

"You offend me," she hissed and turned on her heel, her hair swinging out and nearly smacking him in the face before she stalked back toward her house. "You're replacing it," she called over her shoulder.

He didn't respond because he was too busy telling his cock to settle the fuck down. Whatever he'd smelled in her house was definitely her and something in him really liked it. He watched until she slammed her front door, then he turned back to his project. It was a coffee table he was making out of a nice light oak.

Aurora couldn't believe the audacity of the man. Not only had he walked *inside* her home uninvited, she wasn't sure if she'd locked the door or not, so she supposed she couldn't accuse him of breaking and entering. But he had stolen and broken something that belonged to her. This was more than neighborly rivalry. This felt like a major escalation of their banter. She picked up her phone and called her dad.

"Hey sugar plum, how are you doing? Do you know if you're pregnant yet?" Lionel Patchell asked and she instantly calmed. He was a soothing and solid presence in her life, and he never judged or controlled. She loved him.

"No, I don't know yet and I feel normal. I called to ask a question actually. Can I have my neighbor arrested for stealing my coffee table?"

Her father laughed, a deep rumbling sound that reminded her of summer days and campfires. "What did you do?"

"Me?" she scoffed and paced her now much roomier living room. "I might have taken his plant."

"Sweetie, you need to leave that poor boy alone."

"He is not a boy," she said under her breath remembering how his sweaty chest and stomach had been speckled with sawdust and glinted in the sun. There was a light trail of dark hair that led from his belly button to the top of his jeans she'd been unable to keep her gaze from following. "He's a man, and a menace."

"And you never do anything to provoke that menace, do you?" he teased.

"I still think he should be talked to about appropriate behavior."

"You know, I think I'll let you two deal with this one. I wouldn't want to have to arrest my daughter for plant theft."

"You're supposed to always be on my side."

"Would you feel better if I came out there this weekend to threaten him?"

She knew he wasn't serious about the threatening part, but she always loved to see her dad. "Yes, I would. I'll make you lunch on Sunday."

They said goodbye and she hung up feeling a little better. Her dad was always a reasonable influence on her, which is why she called him instead of her mother or Claire when she was really worked up about something. She knew she needed to stop acting like a child, she was going to *have* a child, maybe, probably. So she would give up the immature vendetta she had against her neighbor and then he'd have no reason to reciprocate.

She couldn't be held responsible for actions taken if he acted out first however, that was just fair and she was no push-over.

Two days later Aurora found a simple yet beautifully crafted coffee table sitting on her front porch. She squealed in delight and looked over at Onyx's house ready to tell him she accepted his apology. He was nowhere in sight. She figured he didn't want to make a big deal about it since he had left it while she was asleep and he probably didn't expect a thank you anyway. That was good because she didn't want to give one since the only reason he'd done it was because he'd destroyed hers to begin with.

She dragged the solid piece of furniture inside and stared at it in her living room. It was the perfect size for the space and made her want to commission him to make her new bookcases and end tables. *Damn*, she wished she hated it, but he knew how to work with wood. She had to stop herself from inserting a dirty joke there. Teaching teenagers kept her humor around the level of a seventeen-year-old.

She decided she would thank Onyx for the table in the spirit of a new truce by baking some cookies and leaving them on his porch. That way he would know she appreciated what he'd done to make things right, but he wouldn't be forced into making small talk about it. It was like a double thank you.

She tied on an apron over her shorts and T-shirt, pulled her hair up into a bun and pulled out the ingredients. She didn't need a recipe, she'd been baking since she was ten. As she measured and mixed, she thought about the possibilities growing inside of her and she daydreamed about cooking for her child in the future. She would make special snacks and meals to help the child grow and thrive, but she would also make fun sweet things every now and then. Balance was key. She wondered what they would like. Most children's tastes were things cultivated from how they were raised, so she imagined her child would appreciate fresh fruits and vegetables out of the garden, but would also love a warm gooey chocolate chip cookie out of the oven. No meat would pass their lips before they were old enough to make that decision for themself. Aurora had been raised vegetarian like her mother, and her father had respected that wish, always providing vegetarian meals when she was with him. As a teen she'd experimented a little but had found the texture and taste of meat off-putting. She wasn't a strict vegan, she ate dairy and eggs, she just couldn't stomach meat.

She was glad she wasn't going to have to have that conversation with some father figure about their child's diet. She'd dated men in the past who had said that if they had a child they would never force them into such an *unnatural* way of eating. As if there was only one way in the world to get the right kind of protein and vitamins. Obviously, those men hadn't lasted past the getting to know you stage of a relationship. Her recent ex, Trent, had been conscientious of her diet when she cooked for him. However, every time they went out he ordered bloody steaks and talked all through dinner about how much he wished he could eat them every day.

She really should have broken up with him long before he cheated on her, but it was a small town and she hadn't seen anyone better. Honestly she'd been afraid of losing the one decent option she saw. She realized now how stupid that was. Settling in a relationship was always a mistake. Dating after having a kid wasn't going to be any easier she imagined, but any decent guy wouldn't see a child as a dealbreaker anyway.

She scooped dough in little mounds on a cooking sheet and slid it into the oven imagining a little face watching the magic of the oven turn ingredients into a treat. She didn't need a man anyway, she had Claire and her parents for company, and she had battery-operated assistance for when she needed a release.

CHAPTER FIVE

Onyx woke in the middle of the night with a start. Something was terribly wrong, or incredibly right. His body was reacting as if a succubus had her mouth wrapped around his cock but he didn't remember being in the middle of a sexy dream. In fact, he was fairly certain he'd been dreaming that his neighbor was pregnant. He groaned and reached down his body, just to be sure his home hadn't been invaded by a sex-crazed burglar. But all he found was his hard and leaking member. He fisted himself and began to stroke as he tried to hold on to sleep. If he could just get himself off and fall back to sleep that would be ideal. A gust of wind blew the curtains near his head and he inhaled the fresh air he loved, free of city pollutants and not a hint of any other werewolf.

He froze, thumb pressed against the head of his cock as his seed spurted from it in a sudden and surprising burst. The usually fresh clean air carried a smell his wolf knew immediately even if he'd never scented it before.

A female pregnant with *his* child.

A roar ripped through his throat as he came and came,

confusion nearly overwhelming the most intense pleasure he'd ever felt.

As soon as it stopped he rolled out of bed covered in his own come and his legs shaking. He lurched across the small bedroom and tore open the curtains, unwilling to believe what he was smelling.

The moon was new but the darkness was no problem for his werewolf eyes. He spotted Aurora standing in her backyard. She was dressed in a dark green nightgown with her blonde hair loose and flowing down her back. She had a cup lifted to the dark moonless sky and she was mumbling something. He couldn't understand the words because of the blood that was rushing in his ears and pounding through his veins. He stared as she drank from the jar, bent to the ground and touched the earth, mumbled again, and then poured the rest of the liquid from her jar onto the ground.

He must have made a noise because she stood quickly and turned to face him. She narrowed her eyes and flipped him off before strolling back into her house as if she hadn't just ripped his life to pieces.

His eyes tracked her as she moved, his body frozen in disbelief. As soon as she disappeared behind her back door, his wolf panicked. Onyx jumped through his bedroom window, completely nude. His hands and feet started to morph into paws as he landed on the ground. Instinct drove him forward. He couldn't stop and think about what he looked like or what he was doing, he had to get to her. Everything in him was telling him to find and protect the woman who was pregnant with his child. Half changed, he slammed into Aurora's back door, splintering the wood which sliced him in multiple places but he barely felt the sting.

Aurora's terrified scream snapped him back to himself. He was halfway across her kitchen and she was pressed against a wall looking like she was going to faint as her gaze swung from his face to the floor. Blood dripped off of his arms and thighs onto her white tile. What the hell was wrong with him? This wasn't right, she was scared and trembling and it was his fault. This wasn't protecting, this was hurting.

He concentrated on that because it was the only thing he could think to convince his wolf that they had to leave her, no matter her vulnerable condition. He whined, wanting to comfort her and protect her but he knew he couldn't, not like this. He bared his teeth at her in a snarl meant to convince her to stay where she was while he was gone, then he turned and ran from her. As he burst back into the night he finished his shift and bounded into the nearby woods of her property, needing to get away from her scent so he could hope to think reasonably about what he now knew.

His wolf wouldn't let him get far. He had to be close enough to watch for danger. Onyx settled just on the other side of her garden where he could see the hole he'd made in her home. His mind reeled as he tried to figure through everything he now knew.

Aurora, the human woman who was everything opposite of what he might enjoy in a partner, was pregnant with his child. But that didn't make sense, he'd never slept with her and he never slept with anyone without protection. It made no sense, and it couldn't be true. This had to be a mistake. His wolf must be confused, maybe she was pregnant, maybe she was even pregnant by a werewolf, but there was no way it was his. He'd never slept with her, it's not like she could have stolen his sperm in his sleep and inseminated hers—

The thought stopped dead as he realized there was one very real way, as unlikely as it was, that she could be pregnant with his child. He snarled.

Those fucking witches.

It seemed like the most impossible of impossibilities, except he knew that it *was* true because his wolf instincts told him that it was true. That deep and feral part inside of him recognized the scent of a woman pregnant with his child.

He howled up at the sky. He had to get farther away, had to think. He forced himself up and turned away from the one thing he wanted to be closer to than anything in his life. He locked down on his wolf, forced himself to shift back to human form, and ran from her. He could still remember the smell of her fear and that was the only thing that kept his wolf from fighting back. If she was afraid of him, his wolf knew he couldn't have her and now that was all it wanted.

Aurora was shaking as she stared at the hole where her door had been and the drops of blood on her kitchen floor.

She'd never seen something so horrifying in her entire life. She had thought she was going to die as a midnight snack for her asshole neighbor when he busted through her door. Onyx hadn't been fully in wolf form but in some sort of in between that she'd never in her life witnessed and was wholly more terrifying. He was mostly hairless aside from the top of his head and a little creeping down his back and up his clawed hands and feet, which were shifted into more animal than man. The rest of him had been an emaciated, stretched out, and downright painful looking version of his normal body. It didn't help that he had been bleeding from the crash through her door. But his face, that had been the most frightening of all. Huge yellow eyes, elongated snout, and sharp teeth that were enormous in his still mostly human looking mouth. It was a face to inspire nightmares, and she would surely never forget it.

Aurora slumped to the floor when she heard his howls getting further away, then she started to shiver as the adrenaline slowed and left her cold.

She wasn't sure how long she sat there but eventually she picked herself up and grabbed her phone, but who should she call? He hadn't harmed her, so calling the police seemed like an overreaction. He wasn't still here threatening her, either. Something told her that he wasn't going to come back and harm her. There had been a look in his eyes the moment before he turned and left, a clarity and a sadness. She didn't know what the hell was going on, but she didn't think he *wanted* to hurt her. She put her phone back down. She would figure it out in the morning. If he'd gone feral there was surely someone who took care of that sort of thing. If he was just being an asshole, well then maybe she *should* call the police and have them come talk to him about it, but not tonight.

She got her gun. She didn't usually feel like she needed it, but tonight she was grateful that her father had insisted she own and know how to use a firearm. She loaded it, made sure the safety was on, then crawled into bed and set it on her nightstand within easy reach. If he came in again she wouldn't hesitate to at least threaten him with it.

She didn't fall right to sleep. The distant sounds of howling kept her awake for hours, but finally, as the first rays of sun started to brighten the sky, she fell into a dreamless sleep.

CHAPTER SIX

Aurora woke to the sounds of hammering and the late morning sun lighting up her room. When she remembered why she was sleeping so late the fear of last night filled her again and her eyes went to the gun still sitting on her nightstand. It wasn't too early to call Claire now, but it would take a while for her to get here. Normally she didn't mind living so far from town with only Onyx as her neighbor, but this morning it felt like a potentially deadly miscalculation. She grabbed the gun before slipping on a robe and tiptoeing toward the sounds that were definitely not coming from next door like usual.

She found Onyx in her house. There was a new door leaned up against her dining room table, and most of the debris from last night was already cleared out and he'd even wiped up the blood. He was fully human, dressed in his usual jeans and T-shirt, work boots, and toolbelt. His hair was held up in his usual man-bun and she realized that last night it hadn't been. When she'd first seen him glaring at her out his bedroom window she'd been taken by surprise to see his hair loose and reaching down to his shoulders. She'd never seen it like that and for just a moment she'd found it very attractive. But then she'd remembered he was glaring at her for just existing on her own property and she'd flipped him off. She swept her gaze over his exposed arms and noticed that there was no evidence of last night's injuries on him, he healed fast.

"Are you going to shoot me with that?" he asked, not looking up from where he was knocking out some pieces of the old frame.

Aurora looked at the gun in her hand and decided it probably wasn't necessary. She set it on the counter and crossed her arms over her chest. "What are you doing?" she demanded.

"Fixing this door."

"Why?"

"Because I broke it."

"Why did you break it?" she whispered, hating that her voice shook slightly at the terrifying memory.

He stiffened and stopped his work, finally looking up and meeting her gaze. His eyes were a little yellow and she took a step back, which only seemed to make him angry. His gaze narrowed and he practically snarled. "Don't run," he warned.

She hadn't been planning to, but now that he told her not to, she wanted to do nothing more.

"Why did you break my door last night?" she asked again, proud of her strong voice. "If you wanted more cookies you could have just brought my plate back and asked nicely," she said in a teasing tone she didn't really feel.

"You're pregnant."

She stiffened. "Not that it's any of your business, but I hope to be. I don't know for sure yet." She touched her stomach and frowned, did werewolves hate pregnant women?

"You *are* pregnant," he said again; a statement not a question, she realized.

"Is this some kind of weird werewolf thing? You can smell the fetus and you want to feast on it or something?" She searched her mind for any mention of werewolves and behavior around pregnant women.

"Did you go to the Stonecroft clinic in Oceanview and get inseminated?"

"Did you snoop around when you were in here stealing my table, asshole?" she demanded. It was the only way he could know, if he'd seen a pamphlet or something maybe.

"You're not denying it."

"No," she defended. "I'm not ashamed of the fact that I took control of my life and how and when I get pregnant. If you're going to tell me I shouldn't be raising a kid on my own you can fuck right the hell off."

His eyes darkened. "You went to the clinic where I left my sperm."

"So? I didn't pick your cranky sperm, why the hell would I pick werewolf sperm?"

"I can smell what is growing inside your womb, Aurora. That's my child in there."

"That's not possible," she whispered, wrapping her arms around her middle protectively. If she was pregnant she wanted to celebrate, but if she was pregnant with *his* child ... she wasn't sure how she felt about that.

He had the audacity to roll his eyes at her. "Anything is possible where witches are concerned."

"Is that why you ran here ready to murder me last night?"

"I wasn't trying to murder you."

She threw her arms down at her sides and stepped forward, glaring at him. She was thankful for the distraction from his revelations about her possible child. "You still ruined my door. I could call the police for what you did." She eyed her phone which was plugged in on the counter. She wasn't likely to shoot him, but she could make a phone call and have the sheriff here within fifteen minutes.

"Probably," he agreed and went back to work.

"So maybe you should start giving me more answers if you want to stay out of the pound," she snapped.

That caught his attention. He threw his hammer down and stepped toward her. "Listen to me very carefully, Aurora. You are pregnant, you went to that fucking clinic in Oceanview and you were inseminated." He took an obvious deep breath as he got closer to her and it felt somehow intimate. "You picked my sperm," he growled, his gaze running down to her stomach.

"No, I picked a human, I would never pick a werewolf," she insisted again. "I didn't even have access to the werewolf pages, why would I?"

He stepped forward and leaned in so close his nose practically touched her cheek as he sniffed. "I know what I am smelling, Aurora. What woke me from sleep last night because it was wafting through my window. You are pregnant, and that baby is *mine*." The last word was a low growl that sent a sharp spike of something uncomfortable down her spine. He leaned back and met her gaze, daring her to deny it.

"Fuck that," she hissed, her voice shaking. She moved around him and rushed to get her phone. She would settle this right now. She dialed the Stonecroft Clinic and avoided looking at the infuriating man while it rang.

"Stonecroft Fertility, how may I help you?" the perky receptionist answered.

"This is Aurora Port and I need to talk to Felicity Stonecroft immediately, it's an emergency."

"Oh dear, maybe you should hang up and dial nine-one-one."

"It's not that kind of emergency," she gritted.

"Well, in that case can I get your number and the reason for your call. She'll get back to you as soon as possible."

Aurora's hand was gripping the phone so hard she thought it might crack. "No, I need to know, right now, if she inseminated me with the sperm I picked, or with asshole werewolf sperm."

"Okay, well, wow, that's a new one for me. I can understand your distress, let me pull up your file."

The woman didn't sound as taken aback as Aurora would have expected and that filled her with concern. She walked into her bedroom while she waited, the sound of Onyx getting back to work on the door was a grating reminder that this wasn't a nightmare.

"Here we are," the receptionist said brightly, coming back on the line. "It looks like you were given … oh, oh yes. It seems that Felicity has notated the *Divine Intervention and Chaos Clause* in your file. Under the advisement and request of the Moon Goddess you were in fact given sperm left by a werewolf," she said as if she were happily solving a mystery instead of ruining Aurora's future.

"Tell Felicity to call me," Aurora managed through a tight throat. Her face was hot, and she wanted to throw up. She dropped her phone on the bed and stared at it as if she could force it to rewrite that entire conversation.

"Are you okay?" Onyx's voice surprised her. She hadn't even realized the sounds of his hammering had stopped, but now he was standing in the doorway to her bedroom. He was a large man, and he filled the space, making her feel trapped. "Aurora?" he asked.

His soft tone was something new and it threw her off enough that she was able to let go of some of her panic. "I called the clinic. Moon Goddess," she said in explanation.

Onyx grunted as if it made perfect sense.

"Why aren't you angry?" she asked, confused by his calm reaction. He hadn't been calm last night when he had apparently figured this all out. It had felt like he wanted to kill her because she was pregnant with his child. Those feelings couldn't just disappear overnight. Was she in danger with him for the next nine months? She'd never paid much attention to werewolf family dynamics. Were they a species where the fathers wanted to eat the young because they saw them as competition?

"It's too late to be angry, what's done is done," he said.

She glared at him, *what's done is done?* Was he insane? Yes, actually, she did think he was insane, and she knew she needed to do some research.

"I think you should leave," she insisted.

"I will, but I'm fixing the door first. It isn't safe to have a missing door out here. A wild animal could get in."

He walked away as if the irony in his statement didn't even register in his thick brain.

Aurora gaped after him for a moment, then texted her mom and Claire. She needed help, advice, and most of all, comfort.

CHAPTER SEVEN

Claire arrived first, since she lived in town, and she came armed with extra tissues and doughnuts. They sat on the front porch so Onyx couldn't hear them and Aurora only cried a little as Claire did emergency googling of werewolf lore. Thankfully they couldn't find anything to indicate Onyx was a danger to her or the child. In fact it seemed like he would be super protective of them both, she'd bet he would hate feeling that way towards her at least.

Aurora cried on Claire's shoulder as realization of the situation settled over her. She wasn't sure if her tears were of joy because she was likely pregnant, or of frustration because her pregnancy had been hijacked by the Moon Goddess and her frustrating neighbor.

Her mother arrived looking like she'd just walked from the garden, which she probably had. She wore a bright orange sundress under an apron that Aurora knew would have pockets full of seeds and cuttings. She loved how predictable her mother was and when Bea pulled Aurora into her arms and the familiar scent of dirt and patchouli surrounded her, she felt like everything would be okay.

Bea pulled back and grabbed her daughter's face. "You look like a woman who is capable of anything," she said. It was what her mother always greeted her with, ever since she was a child. The words of affirmation were everything Aurora needed in that moment.

"I am," she agreed with a shaky breath.

"Good, let's make some tea and lunch," she said, rightfully assuming that Aurora hadn't eaten anything other than doughnuts yet. "Claire my dear," she said then, turning to greet the other woman on the porch. "I am so glad you were here so quickly to support Aurora with exactly what she needed. You are a good friend and a brilliant woman."

Claire hugged Bea, beaming at the praise and they went inside together. Aurora was glad to see that Onyx was done replacing the door and had cleaned up so well it was nearly impossible to tell that anything traumatic had happened the night before. If it wasn't for the need to touch up some paint around the new door and the fact that her once bright blue door was now a boring white, she might be able to pretend it hadn't happened.

"Well that's a nice door, much stronger than the one that was there before," her mother said as she inspected it.

"Onyx did a great job so fast," Claire added.

"Well, *he* broke it, so he was obligated to fix it," Aurora pointed out.

"And you said he made you a coffee table too?" Claire asked.

"Again, because he broke mine," Aurora huffed as she followed the two into the living room to examine the table in question.

"Wow, he's hot *and* handy," Claire giggled as she admired the piece. She'd always been vocal about appreciating Onyx's form and although Aurora had always agreed with her friend on the man's looks, she'd never agreed with her friend's desire to hit on him. Now she had a weird feeling she didn't want to examine when thinking about her best friend complimenting Onyx.

Thankfully the couple of times that Claire had ventured over and tried to push her breasts in Onyx's face he'd merely grunted and ignored her. To be honest, Aurora kind of liked Onyx for that. She wasn't trying to cunt block her friend, but she really didn't want to know anything about Onyx's sex life either and Claire liked to share details.

"I guess we should celebrate," her mother said, and went back to the kitchen and began pulling ingredients out of Aurora's fridge.

"What exactly are we celebrating?" Aurora grumbled.

"You're pregnant, it worked. You're getting what you want and I'm going to be a grandma."

"And I'm going to be an aunt," Claire squealed. "We can't have champagne, can we? I guess I should have brought sparkling cider."

"I can't take a test for another two weeks," Aurora pointed out, trying to calm the two down. They were runaway trains on their own, she should have thought twice about inviting them over together today for sympathy and a grounded opinion.

"No need for that now, is there? A werewolf mate can detect pregnancy far sooner than any test could. Not to mention if the Moon Goddess is involved then things are pretty certain," her mother pointed out.

"*Mate?* Oh no, there is no *mating* involved here, Mom." Just the thought of letting that monstrous man anywhere near her intimately made her want to scream, especially now. She wasn't sure she'd ever be able to get over what he'd looked like as he'd broken through her door.

"Don't you know anything about werewolf culture, Aurora?" Claire said. "Werewolves are obsessed with family and they mate for life." She spoke as if it were the most romantic thing in the world rather than an instinctual trap.

"It's a wonder that he would have donated his sperm in the first place," her mother added. "They are extremely protective and particular about who has their children. They usually want their one chosen mate to bear them many children."

Aurora stopped paying attention as her mother started talking about a werewolf family she'd known on a commune in Utah. Claire was entranced by the story that Aurora had heard multiple times growing up.

Aurora's mind circled around what her mother had said about male werewolves being so particular, it was pretty much what Claire had looked up online too. She'd always wondered why Onyx was out here without a pack and she'd never seen him with a date, male or female. When she'd first moved in she'd had her father look him up just in case he was on the run from the law. It had just seemed too weird that he was young and seemingly healthy, not an ancient curmudgeon as she'd expected. But there were no outstanding warrants and although she was never able to confirm he wasn't gay, there had been no confirmation of any sexual preference because the man didn't date at all. He also didn't have friends and didn't interact with anyone unless it was absolutely necessary.

"Did you do the new moon ceremony last night?" Her mother asked in a way that told Aurora it wasn't the first time she'd tried to get her attention. Claire was looking at her with a raised eyebrow as well.

"Oh, yeah, that's why I was outside at midnight."

"Wonderful. Well with all signs pointing to a healthy and happy pregnancy and birth, I think we should start planning the baby shower," Bea said with a happy clap of her hands.

Claire squealed in excitement. "Yes! Oh, and a gender reveal, those are really important nowadays."

Aurora gave her mother and Claire both a stern look, "No."

"Why not?"

"Because women don't have baby showers until they are huge and uncomfortable and wishing for anything to distract them from the horrors that persist in the last few weeks of pregnancy.

And as far as a gender reveal, well I haven't even decided if *I* want to know the gender."

"You've been listening to too many women at work complain. Pregnancy is beautiful and wonderful," her mother assured her.

"Then why did you only do it once?" she challenged.

"Because you were so perfect I knew I couldn't possibly have another, it wouldn't compare."

Aurora rolled her eyes at her mother. She'd heard that story before too, and she knew it was bullshit but her mother refused to tell her the truth. It bothered Aurora that even now she was holding back.

"I promise you two can throw me a baby shower when it's time."

That seemed to appease the two enthusiastic women.

They spent the remainder of the afternoon together dreaming up ridiculous baby names and discussing the possibilities of nursery themes. Claire wanted pirates for a boy or mermaids for a girl, Bea thought it should be fairies no matter the gender. By the time they left, Aurora was feeling hopeful and blessed. And also confident that she definitely wasn't asking them to help her decorate the nursery when it was time.

She was going to be a mother. And no matter if the baby was half werewolf, she was going to love it and raise it and she was going to have this dream come true in her life.

Onyx forced himself to work so he wouldn't go back over and check on Aurora. His wolf was loud in his head and it was nearly impossible to ignore the thoughts that kept circling through his mind. The female carrying his child was unprotected and unclaimed. Any other male could walk up to her and woo her at any time. Any other male could try and take what was his.

"No," he growled. She wasn't his and he didn't want her to be his. She was annoying and chipper. She was the embodiment of the sun and he was a child of the moon. They were opposites in every way, completely incompatible.

She was pregnant with his child.

He was tempted to go to that clinic and demand ... demand what? He had no right to want them to undo what they did. He had given up all rights to the sperm when he'd sold it to them. But he had never expected this. The sperm should have been used years ago, given to a werewolf woman who had a mate who, for whatever reason, couldn't get her pregnant. This was so far outside of what he would have expected, and he couldn't handle it.

He didn't want a child. He definitely didn't want Aurora. But Aurora was having his child, and that confused everything for him.

Onyx realized he had sanded a piece of wood so far down it was uselessly thin. He threw it against the wall of his shop and was satisfied by the sound of it splintering. His carefully constructed existence was doing the same, so it felt incredibly right.

He leaned over his work bench and tried to settle his swirling thoughts. What was he even supposed to do? She had to know that it would be impossible for him to ignore the fact that she was having his child. She had to know that there were now expectations on him, drives from his wolf that were impossible to ignore.

She had to know that she was now and forever bound to him whether she liked it or not. Just as he was bound to her and their child. He would do anything to protect them and that scared the shit out of him.

He tried to push those spiraling thoughts away and refocus on his work. He grabbed a new piece of wood to sand down into an armrest for a rocking chair.

Aurora's mother surprised Onyx by walking over to his open garage.

"So you're going to be Aurora's baby daddy," she said in a tone that told him she was teasing.

He did not appreciate the levity.

She was a tall woman, much like Aurora, and still quite pretty despite her age. She was an old hippie, and it showed in her appearance. Her long greying blonde hair was in two braids and she had not a swipe of makeup on her face, which did have just a few earned wrinkles and plenty of sun spots.

Her intelligent blue eyes assessed him and he found himself straightening his spine, hoping she approved of what she saw.

"Unintended," he muttered.

"I know. Aurora tells me everything." She narrowed her eyes, accusing. "So tell me, Mr. Werewolf, do I need to be worried that you are going to do something violent?"

"No," he rushed to assure her. "I didn't mean to scare her last night. I could never harm the woman carrying my child. It surprised me, that's all, and I reacted without thinking. I wouldn't have harmed her, my wolf wants to ... protect her."

She nodded as if she'd expected that exact response. "My mother told me you were a quiet neighbor. That you minded your own business but that you had told her once that if she ever needed anything she could call on you and you'd be right there to assist. I appreciated knowing someone was close by that could help an old woman out if needed. It gave me comfort as she aged and allowed me to let her stay where she wanted until she died."

Onyx sort of hated that this woman knew so much. It felt like a violation of sorts, that these women had been so into sharing. He didn't respond, just waited for what she wanted to say next.

"I am withholding judgement on you. I assume you know who Aurora's father is."

Of course he did, her police officer father had driven out in his patrol car the week she'd moved in. Onyx was almost certain it was a statement to him and anyone else around that Aurora was well protected. Onyx could respect the statement, same as he could respect this one that her mother was making now.

Aurora had a family that would protect her, she had a pack.

"I'll take your silence for acknowledgement. I look forward to getting to know you better, Mr. Werewolf."

"Onyx," he said.

"I know, and my name is Bea."

"You were named after your mother," he said, surprised.

"I was. She hated her husband so much she wanted to curse him twice, so she made sure she birthed a girl and named me after herself."

Onyx smiled at the bit of knowledge about his dead neighbor. She'd been a spicy old woman and this fit perfectly.

"Aurora isn't like her. She's not hard," Bea said seriously. "Don't hurt her."

Onyx watched the woman walk away knowing she wasn't talking about physical harm and Onyx had no intention of getting close enough to do any emotional damage to Aurora.

That night when Aurora's house was dark and quiet and had been for an hour, he let his wolf take over. He shifted and made his way around her property line, marking her property more thoroughly. Nothing would dare pass that line he'd pissed in the dirt, not unless they wanted their throat ripped open.

Satisfied that he'd done what he could, he went home and to bed with his window open, hoping that he'd catch the scent of her on the breeze.

Onyx dreamed of twenty years ago.

"It is your duty," his father roared at him across the dining table.

"No, it's just what you want me to do. I am my own person, I'm not an extension of you," Onyx seethed. It was the same conversation they'd had too many times and it had always ended the same, but not this time. Onyx was done making life decisions based on what his father wanted

him to do. *"I will never marry someone I don't love, no matter what you think is best."*

"You are a disgrace to this family and your brother's memory, Onyx. I don't want to see your hide in my territory again if you can't be a man and do your duty to that girl, she's part of this pack."

"That girl is a bitch and a liar, and I refuse to be tied down to her."

Onyx barely saw his father move, but he felt the sting of his punch.

Onyx gasped and sat up in bed, sweat pouring off his body and his heart pounding. He hated that dream, and it haunted him at least once a month.

He fell back onto the bed and Peggy jumped up to cuddle with him. "Did I scare you?" he cooed at her.

He stroked her fur and replayed the rest of that day in his mind. It was the last time he saw his father or any of his siblings. He'd packed his belongings and took off because he refused to live a life his father controlled. Onyx had spotted Rebecca on his way down the drive. She was standing next to her family's small cabin that was on the edge of his own family's property. She glared as he passed, she must have guessed that he had chosen to leave rather than take on the responsibility of her and the child she was carrying. A child he had every reason to believe wasn't even his brother's. Not that his dad seemed to care, all that man cared about was the image of the family and assuring that someone carried on in his footsteps.

Onyx wasn't going to be that for him and as unfair as it was, he resented his brother for dying and putting him in the position to be next in line.

CHAPTER EIGHT

"No dad, I don't think he's dangerous," Aurora repeated as she dished up the vegetable lasagna she'd made for him.

Lionel Patchell's green eyes assessed her from beneath thick dark brows and his mustache twitched. He didn't take any chances when it came to her and she appreciated it. "I'm going to do another background check."

She'd known he would. "I don't think it will help. You found nothing interesting three years ago and he's still a very private person. Didn't you say he comes from a wealthy family and a small pack?"

"From what I could find, yes. No living parents and apparently no contact with the remaining family or pack. Psychopaths tend to be loners," her father grumbled. "Does your mother know?"

"Yes, I had her over on Friday and we talked."

"She isn't worried?"

"Nope, she is thrilled," Aurora said as she rolled her eyes.

He chuckled. "Your mother likes everyone. Well, I'll let you know when I get the results of the background check. I am also going to make sure there are no outstanding complaints about that clinic. They shouldn't have been able to switch your chosen sperm like that, seems illegal." He took a bite of the lasagna and made appropriately appreciative sounds. She knew he would have preferred meat in it, but he was always a good sport when they were together.

Aurora took a bite, it was good. "Apparently there was a clause, something about the Moon Goddess." Aurora hadn't had a chance to look too far into that and it seemed like a pointless worry now. The damage was done and the last thing she wanted to waste her energy on was suing the place that had given her a child. She also would never want her child to grow up and think they weren't wanted or a mistake. But she knew her father wouldn't feel good about not looking into it for her.

"I'll talk with a lawyer friend of mine. Do you have a digital copy of the forms you could send me later?"

"I think so."

"Even with all that, you know I love you, right? And no matter what, I am very excited to be a grandpa."

She felt herself glow at his acceptance. She knew this child was going to have so many people to love it and that was part of why she didn't mind raising it without a father. Except was she raising it without a father anymore? She didn't know what to expect from Onyx now, and that made her uncomfortable.

They finished dinner and dessert which was peach pie that her father had brought with him. Then he gave her hugs and kisses and promises to talk soon after he investigated Onyx again. She waved at him from the front porch but he didn't head to his car, he crossed the property line and headed toward the open garage and the sounds of Onyx working. Great, she hoped her father didn't threaten the man. A part of her kind of hoped he did though because if Onyx kept breaking things at her house she'd have to accept that she was in an abusive relationship, minus the relationship.

· · ·

Onyx hadn't planned to be working in the garage all evening but he had seen Officer Patchell pull up and expected a visit so he'd stayed out working to make it easier. The last thing he wanted to do was have a conversation with the man in his doorway or invite him inside his house. As expected, Lionel walked over with a look on his face that Onyx was certain he used when approaching loitering teens.

It was a good look. Onyx felt his heartrate speed up and he wanted to start apologizing even though he'd done nothing wrong.

"Onyx West," Lionel said.

"Officer Patchell."

"I never had a problem with you living out here next to my daughter and I know Beatrice talked fondly of you, but that doesn't mean I can't change my mind. I am not only an officer of the law, but I am Aurora's father. If you do anything to make her uncomfortable again I will be taking it as my personal duty to see your life here is impossible."

"Understood," Onyx said. He had no argument, no defense. If he was in Lionel's position he'd be doing the same thing. It's how a father was supposed to protect his children.

Aurora was lucky she had two parents who cared so deeply for her.

"Great, have a nice evening," Lionel said and walked away.

Onyx looked over at Aurora's house and saw her watching him from her living room window. She looked nervous. Had she expected an altercation? Did she really think so little of him? As if he'd pick a fight with the grandfather of his child.

He wondered what his own father would have thought of this situation. He'd probably disown Onyx all over again. He figured his surviving siblings would be neutral about the situation and his friends … well he had none to speak of so it was silly to think about. But if he had kept in touch with his best friend since childhood, he imagined Glen would be supportive because he wasn't an asshole. Onyx felt a tightness in his chest realizing he had no one to share this news with. Whether he felt it was good news or bad, he was alone in it and for the first time in all these years he felt like that was a lonely thing.

So far he knew Aurora had told Claire, her mother, and her father. She wasn't waiting or hiding from this situation. Was she happy about it? She'd obviously gotten pregnant on purpose, but she certainly hadn't picked his werewolf sperm on purpose. He'd expected more tears than she'd spilled with Claire and possibly signs of depression. But she was going about her life like normal. She'd spent yesterday in her garden and this morning he'd watched her mow the lawn and water the wolfsbane that separated their yards, same as she did every Sunday during summer. It confused him.

She also hadn't acknowledged him any more than usual. Did she think that she was going to go on about her life as if that baby wasn't his?

That thought had his body heating in anger. She couldn't be that stupid, could she? She couldn't think that he'd just sit across the yard from his child and not know it, not acknowledge it or love it.

Love it ... *fuck*, he knew he was going to love it. He could feel that bond forming even now. It was something that was unique to werewolves, this bond a father had with a child even while it was in the womb. It was why werewolf fathers stayed so close to their mates throughout pregnancy and often opted to deliver the baby themselves rather than let someone else be the first to touch it.

Would Aurora even let him in the room when she gave birth? He had so many questions and no idea how to talk to her about any of them. He went inside and googled human pregnancy and birth customs and was horrified to see the pages of father comments about how they didn't even feel like the child was theirs until they saw it and held it the first time, often after it was washed and wrapped. It was as if they were completely separated from the experience their wives and girlfriends were going through. What a sad thing for them. If this was what she was raised to expect, it made Onyx wonder and worry that Aurora would be unable to understand what he felt and wanted.

He was going to have to talk with her. They were going to have to work out some kind of understanding and expectations. The sooner the better too because not being able to go check on her regularly was making him anxious.

CHAPTER NINE

Aurora couldn't spend another day at home. It had been a week since she'd gotten Onyx's wolfy pregnancy affirmation and she hadn't felt like going anywhere as the new reality settled around her. Today she was ready to move forward so she was going to head into town and do a little shopping and socializing. She was also going to pick up a pregnancy test because there was still a part of her that wanted that definitive little line. She was a week early on recommended testing, but she knew that it could already be positive. Maybe she'd buy two just in case. She dressed in a pink summer dress, braided her hair in one long thick braid and grabbed her purse. She headed to her car with a spring in her step.

As soon as she closed her car door, the passenger door swung open making her jump and scream. Onyx was leaning in with a scowl.

"What are you doing?" he demanded.

She held one hand to her chest like she was fighting off a heart attack and glared at the culprit. "Going to town, not that it's any of your business," she snapped and buckled her seatbelt.

"Why?"

She started the car and shook her head. What the hell was his deal? Did he think he had a right to track her? She stopped that thought because she was sure she knew the answer and she didn't like it. He'd been watching her more closely since the night he broke her door down. He wasn't talking to her, but he was definitely watching, and she'd chosen to ignore it. *Now* he wanted to talk? When she was on her way to do something?

She decided that the best approach with him was the same she took with her students who wanted to throw attitude her way— calm and reasonable. Unfortunately, if that didn't work she couldn't call in the principal to back her up.

"I need to pick up a few things," she explained. "Is there something I can grab for you while I'm there?" she asked in her cheeriest drawl. "Perhaps some soap?" she said wrinkling her nose dramatically. In truth he smelled amazing, his scent was a mix of wood and man, he'd obviously been working before running over to stop her from leaving.

He didn't answer, just dusted off a bit then got in the passenger seat and closed the door.

Aurora gaped at him. "What the fuck are you doing?" she demanded, done with being nice.

"I need to go to town too. We should save gas, I know you care about the environment," he said as he grabbed the seatbelt. He was trying for nonchalant, she could tell, but the way his knees pressed against the dashboard and how he was fighting to stretch the rarely used seatbelt across his wide body had her lips lifting in mirth.

Well, if he wanted to come along and play bodyguard or whatever, fine, she would let him this time. She backed out of the driveway just as he was lifting the lever on the seat and pushing the back, which made him end up sliding forward again and smashing his knees against the glovebox.

"Oops," she whispered.

He cursed and she smiled as she put the car in drive and sped forward, sending him shooting back as he lifted the lever to adjust again.

"What the fuck is wrong with this seat?" he growled, and she couldn't hold back the laugh.

"I think it's user error, honestly."

He glared at her, but she ignored it.

"I think it's driver error," he snarled.

She just shrugged and rolled down her window, turned the music up, and drove without saying another word to him. He may have inserted himself into her life, but she didn't have to let him know she cared. If they had been normal friendly neighbors this sort of outing might be a regular thing. Sharing a ride into town for weekly shopping or even chatting. They weren't normal friendly neighbors though, and having him so close to her in the car was making her body tingle with an awareness of him that she thought she'd gotten over the first time he opened his mouth.

She tried to remind herself of what an asshole he was. She pictured her smashed coffee table and door. That helped until he lifted his ass slightly off the seat and adjusted his crotch in what he surely thought was a smooth unnoticeable move. She watched from her periphery like it was the beginning of a bad porn and her body started tingling all over again. Images of the day she'd met him filled her mind. This was no time for her masturbation reel, she was driving, and he was far too close to her. Her body wasn't listening though and she squeezed her thighs together as a familiar need began to grow.

He snapped his head in her direction and his eyes widened, then he rolled down his window. He moved so close to the opening she thought he was about to stick his head out and maybe hang his tongue too.

When they got to the edge of town she asked him where he needed to go and he just shrugged so she headed to Main Street. It was a small town and there were only a few places most people went regularly, and they were all within walking distance.

Onyx jumped out of the car even before she had it in park, as if he couldn't get away from her fast enough. She was tempted to point out that she hadn't invited him along and he was welcome to walk home. It seemed like he was maybe trying to form a friendship of sorts though, so she swallowed the remark.

"I'm heading into Jordan's for some flowers," she said, thrusting a thumb in the direction of the town's greenhouse and nursery.

"Me too," he said, his gaze daring her to challenge him on that.

"Okay ..." she said and started walking. She could feel his presence behind her but he didn't try and walk next to her like a friend might, which made it weird. It felt like being followed by a large dog that you weren't sure was friendly and its intention was to protect you, or follow you somewhere quiet to devour you.

Over the last few years she'd gotten to know nearly every resident of the town and usually whenever she walked anywhere she was stopped by friends, students, parents, and acquaintances all wanting to say hello. Today all she got were quick greetings and curious looks at the man behind her. A few people asked her if she was *doing alright* as if it were an unspoken code to see if she was currently under some kind of threat from Onyx. She imagined he was near growling behind her. She doubted he was used to so much attention.

"I'm doing well. I just had to come into town for a few things and Onyx needed something so we decided to carpool. It's better for the environment and Onyx is very conscientious," she said in explanation, gaining politely doubtful murmurs in return. No one seemed prepared to press the issue further though, something she was both grateful for and annoyed about. What if she really was in some kind of danger? Was no one willing to step between her and the beast that was her neighbor?

By the time they got to the greenhouse Aurora was ready to tell Onyx to wait outside so she didn't have to have more of the same frustrating interactions. But he hurried forward and opened the door for her. She was so surprised by the act of chivalry she said nothing as he followed her right inside.

"Good morning, Aurora. Are you looking for anything special today?" Gertrude Jordan asked from behind a row of potted raspberry bushes. She was short and fit, likely from lifting and moving heavy potted plants and bags of soil all day. She had short grey hair that she tucked behind her ears and her skin was bronzed from the sun. The wrinkles on her face and the wisdom in her blue eyes spoke of her age. Those knowing eyes drifted over her to Onyx without surprise or concern. "Onyx, I have that fertilizer for you, it just came in this morning. I was going to give you a call, but it looks like you read my mind."

"Thank you Gertrude. I'll come back for it later with my truck, I don't want to smell up Aurora's car."

Aurora was surprised by the friendly way Gertrude talked to Onyx, but when he responded in an equally friendly tone she'd never heard him use before, she was left stunned.

Gertrude turned to Aurora and raised a brow as if by that one comment of his she'd ascertained everything that was happening in their lives. Which maybe she had, Aurora knew the woman was a witch, maybe she was clairvoyant too.

Aurora shook herself out of her stupor over the entirely uncanny interaction. "It's okay, we can stick it in the trunk. I'm hoping to pick up a few plants to fill my front porch pots."

"I'll show you the best ones for that," Gertrude said. "Onyx, your bags are in the back, you know what to grab."

Aurora followed Gertrude, still bewildered by this woman's apparent ease with the man the rest of the town treated like a monster. The only thing she could reason was that because Gertrude was the only other supernatural in the small town, the two had bonded over it. Most places, ever since the supernaturals came out, had either no supernaturals, or entire clans. She wasn't sure what it was about Greensferry that made it a magnet for loners, but the town had these two, and that was it. There was a large vampire coven nearby, but it was not considered part of the town and Greensferry residents never really interacted with them.

If she were being honest, it made her feel bad for Onyx that he was treated so poorly by everyone. *She* knew he wasn't a monster. He was an asshole, sure, but he wasn't a monster. She'd never felt in danger living near him, aside from the night he splintered her door of course. But everyone in town aside from Gertrude seemed to be waiting for him to attack.

"So you and Onyx are friends?" Gertrude asked after showing her to the right section.

"We are neighbors," Aurora clarified.

"Seems like something else is going on. That boy comes into town twice a month, less if he can help it, and he was here just last week. I expected to have to send those bags up to him by delivery but here he is in my store, with you."

Aurora wasn't sure what to say so she grabbed a couple plants without paying attention to what they were and turned to Gertrude. "I'll take these, thanks."

Gertrude rolled her eyes, then took a pot from her that was something green and very leafy and put it back on the shelf. "That is not what you want, poisonous to cats. Take this one, attracts butterflies when it blooms."

Aurora accepted the proffered plant. "I don't have a cat."

"No? Hm, I could have sworn Onyx said you did and that's why he buys so much catnip."

Aurora followed Gertrude to the counter with a frown. What the hell was Onyx doing with catnip? Surely *he* didn't have a cat, he was a werewolf, don't werewolves eat cats?

A horrible thought came to mind. Did he use catnip to attract cats so he could eat them? She wanted to cry just thinking about it. She'd have to do a little exploring behind his house next chance she got and if she found a patch of catnip back there, she was going to freak out.

She walked to the counter to pay and she froze as the back door opened, her attention was riveted to Onyx as he walked out. He had two large bags of fertilizer, one slung over each shoulder and his arms curled up over them, muscles bulging out of his T-shirt. He didn't even look strained under what had to be an extremely heavy load.

"Your mouth is open," Gertrude whispered and Aurora snapped it shut.

She dug in her purse for her wallet. Her cheeks felt like they were on fire after being caught like that. She should not be ogling her neighbor. She paid and ignored the knowing smirk on Gertrude's face.

Onyx stood waiting for her at the door, holding it open for her as she hurried past. She was tempted to reach out and touch one of his biceps to see if it was as solid as it looked. She'd never thought of herself as having a type, she'd been attracted to and dated men of all degrees of physically fit. But something about seeing what Onyx was so easily capable of made her understand other women's obsession with bulging muscles. It was as if she knew just by looking at the man that he was capable of protecting her from anything, and suddenly that was all that mattered to her libido. She had to talk herself down with a reminder that this was the twenty-first century and they weren't likely to be attacked by a bear or a Viking horde. Muscles weren't the indication of a good mate anymore, intellect, she reminded herself. That is what she had always looked for in a partner because conversation mattered, Onyx was not big on conversation.

CHAPTER TEN

Onyx loaded the bags of fertilizer into Aurora's trunk as she settled her new plants safely into the back seat. The trunk lid was up so he missed the approach of Steven Forester until the man's smooth irritating voice was speaking to Aurora.

"Hey Aurora, nice to see you in town today. I was just heading over for a late lunch at the café, care to join me?"

Onyx hated that voice on a regular day, but knowing it was propositioning Aurora made him want to rip the cords right out of the man's throat. He slammed the trunk far harder than necessary making both Steven and Aurora jump.

"Onyx, what are you doing here?" Steven asked with annoyance.

Here as in near Aurora; Onyx knew what the man meant. Why was *he* with *her*. It was a good question with a great answer, but Onyx wasn't about to let Steven in on it. Onyx glared at the intruding man and fought the urge to bare his teeth in a snarl. He wished he'd touched her, gotten his scent on her to warn off others, of course this dense male wouldn't have been able to recognize the warning.

Aurora looked from Onyx back to Steven who was watching

them both with curiosity. "We are neighbors and we both needed to pick some stuff up from Jordan's nursery," Aurora answered. She also took a step away from Steven while fiddling with her purse in an attempt to make the movement seem natural, but Onyx saw it for what it was. This man made her uncomfortable and that made Onyx angry.

"And we need to be getting back," Onyx said firmly. He didn't care if Aurora had other errands to run, he was going to cut off this interaction.

Aurora looked up at him with surprise. "Oh, yeah, Onyx needs to get back to work. See you around, Steven."

Onyx moved between the two to open Aurora's door for her and shut it once she was sitting. Steven watched the whole thing and a feeling of dread creeped into Onyx. Steven was just a human but there was no mistaking the spark of challenge that entered his eyes at the protective way Onyx was treating Aurora.

Onyx ignored him, not willing to validate the man's challenge with even a harsh look. But as he walked around the car leaving Aurora within clear shot of Steven, a low growl rumbled his chest against his will.

"See you around, Onyx," Steven said with a sly tone. "Next time, you owe me lunch, Aurora," he said and knocked on her window lightly.

"Oh, yeah sure," Aurora said.

Onyx dropped into the passenger seat and growled, "Drive."

Aurora shot him a curious look but didn't argue. She waved at Steven and drove out of town.

Onyx was grateful she didn't question him about any of that, and he knew she had every right to. He also knew he had no right to make demands of her or to change her plans because of his jealousy. She had followed along as if it were completely normal and what they had already decided. That told him that on some level she trusted and respected *him* more than Steven. That made his inner wolf very happy.

"What the hell was that all about?" Aurora demanded when they were safely out of town.

"I don't like that guy."

"I could tell, and he is definitely not my favorite person either but there was something more, wasn't there?"

"It doesn't matter."

"It does when you make me cut my trip to town short over it."

He only felt mildly guilty about that. "Steven is a womanizer. I wouldn't wish him around any female, but especially not the one carrying my child."

"Wow, you just used the word womanizer *and* female in the same sentence. I'm not sure you aren't a geriatric asshole instead of a modern one."

He shot her a glare. "Am I wrong?"

"No, he's a known womanizer and I identify as female. I just think that those words went out of style about thirty years ago." She glanced his way then back out to the road. "Are you older than you look? I thought werewolves aged about the same as humans."

"I am only as old as I look," he assured her.

"Okay, I know that I may be up on the lingo a little better than a recluse werewolf since I'm a teacher and hang with teens all day, so I'll cut you some slack. But dude, don't refer to me as a *female* ever again. Also, Steven dating a lot of people isn't inherently terrible. Some women seek out those types and enjoy a purely sexual relationship with no strings attached, it's fine."

Onyx wanted to explode thinking of her seeking out some random asshole like Steven for sexual satisfaction. "You said you don't like him either," he growled.

"I don't, because he continues to hit on me no matter how many times I reject him. So he's an asshole who thinks he's some kind of alpha male, and *that* is the correct way to call it, old man." She gave him a sly wink.

Onyx had heard of this new trend of humans calling

themselves *alpha males* as if it was something you could just decide to be. Stolen from a false sense of the hierarchy of wolves. It made Onyx want to bite the idiots' throats out.

"Can I call him an asshole?"

"That is always in style," she assured him with a smile that did something unexpected to his body.

He grunted and rolled down the window, he needed fresh air. On the drive to town he'd caught the sweet scent of arousal wafting off her and it had taken everything in him to keep his cock down. Now it was just her fucking smile that had him wanting to tell her to pull over so he could bury himself inside of her.

How the hell was he going to survive this pregnancy with her as nothing more than a friendly neighbor? Did he want to? He certainly didn't want to be involved with *her*, did he? He just wanted to be involved with the woman pregnant with his child, right? That was a distinction that mattered to him, and he knew it would matter to her. She didn't seem like the type who would respond well to a request for some bed play from the man who had made her miserable for years.

But what she didn't know was that he'd watched her walk across the lawn three years ago and his wolf had let loose with a needy howl in his head and his entire body had tuned in to her in a way he'd never experienced before. She was suddenly everything he wanted and it had terrified him. How dare she casually walk into his territory and try to control him with her beauty.

So he'd decided to hate her, it was easier, safer. He'd pushed down and buried every other feeling for her and concentrated on how annoying she was. And it had worked well. He'd managed to believe it except when he was in his wolf form. His wolf never stopped pining for her.

Now things were a mess because there was a child involved and it had given his wolf the strength to be a constant voice of desire inside Onyx. Even if Onyx wanted to deny the desire that raced through him for Aurora, he would never forgive himself for harming the child by being an absent father. He had no expectations that she'd change her mind after three years of antagonistic behavior so he had to keep his desire under control.

When they parked in front of Aurora's house and she was unloading her flowers, Onyx remembered she'd said she had cut her trip short because of him. He didn't want her going back to town without him, partly because she might run into Steven again. Or another man who was less of an asshole and therefore more of a threat to his place in her life.

"If you go into town again, let me know, I will as well," he said, unable to keep the snarl of demand out of his tone.

"You hate town," she shot back suspiciously.

"I hate lots of things that I have to do. Since you're pregnant with my child, I want to accompany you when you leave my territory."

Her eyes narrowed at him. "Yes, Sir," she said mockingly and did a little curtsy. "I'll just stay over here in *my* territory," she added before walking toward her house, laughing to herself.

"Trunk," he growled after her.

She didn't even look back, just hit a button on her keys and the thing popped open so he could grab his fertilizer. At least he had something to keep his mind and body busy while he ignored the way her mocking *sir* had sent an electric shock of need straight to his cock.

Aurora busied herself for the rest of the day. She planted the new flowers in pots, made some oatmeal cookies, and tried very hard not to think about her neighbor.

She couldn't help herself though, because he kept making a hell of a lot of noise over there. He definitely wasn't gardening, no matter that he'd just bought fertilizer.

Annoyed, she eyed the final batch of cookies she was about to slip into the oven and an evil idea came to mind.

Half an hour later she had a plate full of fresh baked cookies and she was on her way over to her noisy neighbor's house.

Maybe she was more than a little annoyed that he'd cut her town trip short. She really did want to have that little pink plus sign to stick in her memory box.

She sashayed across her lawn to his.

Onyx straightened from whatever wood project he had dragged out to his driveway and pushed his safety glasses up on top of his head. There were flecks of sawdust stuck to his sweaty face and his shirt was hanging unbuttoned. His tan and toned chest was on full display and she took in the sight of him with appreciation. His muscles glistened with sweat and she never missed an opportunity to study the spattering of paw print tattoos that crossed his pecs. Her gaze traveled farther south to where an amazing muscular V and a trail of dark hair led into the waistband of his jeans. A bulge there had her throat and her cunt flexing.

"Fuck," she whispered almost tripping as she crossed to him.

"You made me cookies?" he asked, eyeing the plate warily. "Did I thank you for the last batch?"

She didn't trust her voice not to betray her lust so she just held out the plate to him. He grabbed one with a grunt. She almost told him to stop, rethinking her plan, but he shoved the whole thing in his mouth and chewed. It was too late.

His eyes widened and he grabbed another, looking at it. "Oatmeal," he commented and put that one in his mouth as well.

She grinned. "I made these for you, as a thank you for today." She pushed the plate into his hands. "Return the plate whenever and the other you still have. Maybe my blanket too."

"Why?" he asked skeptically, taking the plate and eating another cookie.

"You kept me company on the trip to town," she said brightly and spun around as he shoved another one in his mouth. "By the way, you kept me from getting a pregnancy test, asshole." She lifted both her hands to flip him off behind her. "Have fun with the diarrhea."

She heard the plate drop and started walking faster. She imagined him realizing what that unidentifiable taste was and chasing her down.

"Wolfsbane," he growled just as she crossed onto her own property and bolted up her steps.

She heard his front door slam even before she entered her own house. She didn't regret her choice at all because he really had no right to try and control where she went and when. She threw off her apron and grabbed her purse, then walked out to her car.

"Controlling asshole," she grumbled as she drove away, not quite sure if she was hearing a howl coming from his house or if it was her imagination.

CHAPTER ELEVEN

Onyx cursed Aurora as he laid on his bed with stomach cramps. Sweat was already drenching his body. She'd poisoned him, she had actually poisoned him. He'd immediately forced himself to puke up the cookies but it had been too late. The wolfsbane was in his system and all he could do was wait for it to run through.

He hadn't missed the sound of her car leaving but he was helpless to follow. His wolf howled disagreement. Diarrhea she'd said, if only that was what was about to happen.

When Aurora got home she noticed that Onyx hadn't touched the project in his driveway. The mess of wood and tools was just as he'd left it after eating the cookies. She'd never seen him leave anything like that for longer than it took him to grab another piece of wood or a tool. He was actually a very neat and clean guy, something she'd appreciated about him as a neighbor.

She frowned but figured he was nursing his stomachache like a big baby, typical man. She hurried inside to do what she'd been anxious to do since that morning. She had been drinking water for the whole drive to and from town so she was about ready to burst. She started to rip open the package as soon as she was in the house and ran to the bathroom leaving a trail of cardboard packaging behind her. She'd gotten two tests just in case. She'd take one now but if it was negative she wouldn't freak out, she'd wait until the recommended day and take the other.

She closed her eyes as she peed on the pregnancy test. She wanted this, even if it meant her annoying neighbor was the father. In no small part because there was no way she could afford to try again any time soon.

Three minutes later Aurora was staring at a pink plus sign and tears were streaming down her face. She took a picture and sent it to each of her parents and Claire.

She was officially pregnant and she was ecstatic, terrified, and surprisingly anxious to share this confirmation with Onyx. She immediately got a response from Claire that was all emojis of excitement and babies. Her parents weren't as quick to respond to texts so she set her phone down after sending Claire a smiley face and hearts back.

She gripped the plastic stick tightly as she walked out to her front porch and looked over at Onyx's house. It was quiet and still. Something about that made her uncomfortable. She knew wolfsbane wouldn't kill him, she'd looked it up before she'd decided to plant it between their yards. It was just an annoying smell to werewolves and gave them indigestion if they ate it.

She looked down at the white stick in her hand and then back at his house. They were going to raise a child together and that changed everything.

She had probably overreacted to his overbearing protectiveness, and she'd admit as much to him. But she would also tell him that he needed to ease up on the whole protective thing because she'd lived alone for years and could take care of herself. She wasn't his property, and she didn't live in his territory.

She decided to wave the white flag—or stick—and headed

over to his house. She'd offer to get him some Pepto or saltine crackers if he needed. Then they would talk seriously about how this was going to work best for the child.

She knocked on his door but there was no answer. She knocked again, louder, and she heard a groan.

"Onyx?" she called. "Are you alive?" she asked with a laugh. "Do you need anything?"

Another groan was all she got in response.

She was certain he couldn't die from what she'd done but she decided it was best to just double-check. What if he had an allergy. She opened his door slowly, calling out for him. She had never been in his house before and her eyes swung around to take it all in and hoping to see him lounging and glaring at her. She'd be happy if he shouted at her to get out and leave him alone. There was no sign of him but his place looked comfortable. All the furniture obviously had been made by him and it was rustic but in a chic way that she knew people in the city would pay thousands for. She noticed his scent as she stepped in, it was heavy in the house. She'd only ever gotten little whiffs of it before now and even in the car it hadn't been too strong since she'd had the window down. She liked the smell, a lot. It was earthy and wild, and it made her think of moonlit nights and great sex.

She had to shake herself to remember why she was here, she wanted to make sure she hadn't committed murder by accident. "Onyx?" she called, not as loud this time.

He groaned from the back of the house. The bedroom or bathroom she assumed. A tiny meow caught her attention and a white fluffball came running towards her. She bent down and scooped it up before it could run out the front door.

"Well hello there, what in the world are you doing living with the big bad wolf?" she asked the precious thing, then shut the door and walked slowly toward the back of the house.

The cat began to purr and Aurora was immediately in love.

She passed the open bathroom door and came to a closed door she knew was Onyx's bedroom. She'd figured out the layout of his house long ago and knew his bedroom window looked out at her backyard.

She knocked on the door softly. "Onyx? Are you okay?" she asked through the door.

A groan was all she got in response and a ball of nervousness grew in her stomach. She'd expected him to growl and yell and tell her to get out of his house. Was he really sick? She wished she'd brought her phone instead of her pregnancy test. What if she needed to call for an ambulance? Was she about to be arrested for trying to kill her neighbor? Maybe she should have called her dad for legal advice before coming over here.

"Onyx, I'm coming in," she warned and waited a breath then opened the door when no answer came.

Onyx was curled up on the bed, sweat pouring off his body. His skin looked red and blistered, his hair had fallen mostly out of his usual bun and was so damp it was plastered to his head, face and neck. He was laying on her stolen blanket she realized and a flash of annoyance filled her. She quickly let it go, he could keep the blanket if he just didn't die because of her.

She didn't move closer, afraid he would lash out. "Should I call for help?"

His eyes opened a slit but they didn't seem to be able to focus. "I don't have time for dreams right now," he said, his voice so raspy it sounded painful.

"Do you need to go to the hospital?

"No," he gritted out and then groaned and rolled to his other side showing her his back.

Aurora didn't know what to do, but she knew she couldn't just leave him like this. She ran back to her house and grabbed her phone, only realizing once she was there that she still had the cat in her hands.

"Maybe you should stay here until daddy is better," she cooed at the cat and set it down. She dialed the only person she could think who might know what to do.

"Aurora sweetie, how are you? I saw your text but I'm on duty, congratulations again!"

"I poisoned my neighbor," she blurted.

"Did he try to hurt you?" her father demanded, all trace of celebration out of his tone.

"No, just annoyed me. I made cookies with wolfsbane and he ate a few. Now he's really sick and I'm not sure what to do."

"Let me ask Jason," her father said and the line went quiet as he consulted his partner who was a werewolf. "Jason said that a fever will burn the poison out of him."

"He's got a rash all over."

"That's normal, Aurora," Jason said, her father must have put her on speaker phone. "Is he responding when you talk to him?"

"He did a little, but his voice was real hoarse."

"He likely puked up the cookies when he realized what they were and burned his throat. Best thing you can do is keep him cool and comfortable."

Aurora relaxed, she hadn't killed Onyx. She thanked her father and Jason then hung up. Then she went back to Onyx's house ready to do all she could to alleviate his suffering and hopefully prevent him from killing her when he was better.

CHAPTER TWELVE

Onyx drifted in and out of consciousness, not sure if he was dreaming or awake because both seemed to involve Aurora. She was being sweet and caring which made him think he was dreaming, but then he was sweaty and sick and wanted to die, so he knew he must be awake.

Eventually he woke up to a dark and quiet room. His body wasn't drenched, freezing, or on fire. His stomach felt tender but he didn't want to puke, and his brain seemed to have finally pushed through the fog.

"I can't believe she poisoned me," he growled then regretted it when his throat protested. It was raw from puking and so dry, he needed some water.

Images of Aurora holding a cup to his lips surfaced and he looked over to find the cup sitting on the bedside table. Had she really nursed him through that horrible experience? No one had taken care of him since he was a kid and his mother was still alive. It was almost unbelievable that Aurora of all people had done it now. Of course it was her fault he was sick, so maybe it made perfect sense. Guilt made people do all kinds of things out of character.

Onyx pushed up into a sitting position and frowned as he felt his hair hit his back, but it wasn't loose, it was braided. He reached back and felt it, utterly baffled that she would have taken the time to do something like that for him. He grabbed the glass of water which was thankfully full and drank the whole thing down, wanting more. His movements were slow mostly because he was afraid he was going to suddenly relapse, but eventually he stood. He realized he was still in his jeans but at some point his shoes, socks, and shirt had been removed. He wondered if that had been his doing or Aurora's. Probably hers because if he'd been aware enough to undress then he would have finished the job and been more comfortable.

Stiff and weak from the poison, all he could think about was the fact that he'd be unable to protect Aurora and the baby in this condition. That thought bothered him.

As he shuffled to the kitchen he was startled to find Aurora curled under a throw blanket and asleep on his couch. Why was she here? Why hadn't she gone home to sleep comfortably in her own bed?

A part of him wanted to pick her up and move her to *his* bed where he could curl around her and cover her in his scent. But even if he wasn't too weak to pull that off, he knew he shouldn't do it. She wasn't here to be his mate, she was here because she felt bad for poisoning him. It did alleviate some of his concern over being able to protect her though. No one would dare come into his home to harm her.

He continued into the kitchen and drank two glasses of water then headed for a much needed shower. As he pulled off his jeans it became apparent that he was covered in her scent. It wafted up at him as he moved and he was almost loath to shower it off. Even his hair smelled like her as he released it from the braid she'd created. However, there was also a layer of dried sweat and a feeling of illness that clung to him, that wasn't something he wanted to keep, so he took a long, hot shower.

By the time he was stepping out of the bathroom he was exhausted and wanted to fall back into his bed and sleep for another day, but first he needed to peek at Aurora. He told himself he just wanted to see that she was safe, but he knew that was a lie. He wanted to look at her again and take in more of her scent.

When he got to the living room she was sitting up and waiting for him. There were two cups of tea on the table, and she was looking at him with nerves clear on her face.

"I made you tea," she said, her eyes glued to his face in a way that told him she was trying very purposefully to not look at his naked chest and the thin towel that was separating the rest of him from view. "It's herbal and detoxing."

"Okay," he said.

She seemed surprised as he moved closer to her instead of retreating to dress first and her eyes dipped down his body. The horizon was just starting to brighten, he realized as he sat. It was morning, but of which day he wasn't sure.

"Don't you want to put on clothes?" she asked, her voice a little breathy.

"No, I want to sleep and I usually do that naked."

"Oh," she said, her face turning crimson. "I thought perhaps you were up for the day, you're usually an early riser."

"I am when I'm not recovering from wolfsbane poisoning," he snarled and regretted it when she hunched protectively around herself.

"I'm sorry," she whispered.

He started to take a deep breath but then froze when his senses filled with her and his cock twitched under the towel. "I know," he said and picked up the tea. It smelled terrible but he didn't want to offend her, so he sipped it.

"Are you feeling okay, is there anything you need?"

He needed her to get on her knees and crawl to him, but he didn't think she'd take kindly to that order. The thought made his lip twitch and he took another sip of tea to cover it. His cock however, was not so easily covered and he was thankful she was staring so hard at his face. "It's out of my system, I'm not going to die, don't worry."

"You were pretty out of it for two days," she said.

Two days. That surprised him, she must have used a lot of the horrid stuff. He supposed he was lucky she hadn't called for an ambulance or left him to fend for himself. "Thanks for watching out for me."

"Of course, I was really worried."

He could tell she wasn't lying. She looked like she'd hardly slept for those two days.

"You should go home and rest, I'm fine."

She nodded and stood then wobbled slightly on her feet. He moved fast, catching her as she slumped and blinked her eyes rapidly.

"What's wrong?" he growled, all thoughts of his own weakness and exhaustion fleeing in the face of her illness.

"I think I just stood up too fast."

"When's the last time you ate?" he demanded.

"I'm not sure," she admitted.

He growled and moved her onto the couch. "Don't get up," he demanded then started toward the kitchen.

Her gasp as he walked away is what made him realize the towel hadn't survived his quick movements and she was currently getting an eyeful of his naked ass. He huffed and switched direction, heading to his bedroom to put on some pants. Then he was going to feed her because she was the mother of his child, and if he wasn't taking care of her then he was as shitty a male as his father thought he was.

Seeing Onyx's naked ass had stunned Aurora and she couldn't get her brain back on track. She told herself that was the only reason she was still sitting when he returned to the living room with a pair of sweats on instead of back at her own house. *Dear lord, a half-naked man in sweats is my kryptonite.*

An involuntary *uh* sound escaped that she tried to cover with a cough.

His eyes flashed as if he knew exactly what she was thinking. "You are going to eat. You're pregnant so you can't be skipping meals," he chastised.

"I was a little distracted thinking I'd killed my kid's dad," she snapped back much more comfortable feeling annoyed with this man rather than attracted to him.

"I'm fine and I would have survived without you."

She was hurt by his lack of appreciation, but she should have expected it.

"And I'll survive without you," she said and stood up, feeling better.

"Sit," he commanded in a tone that had her obeying before she could make the conscious decision. "I am going to feed you," he growled.

"Is this like a *wolf* thing?" she asked carefully.

"Yes," he said quietly.

She wasn't sure if that's all it was or what it even really meant, but she wasn't going to argue that she wasn't hungry. She stayed seated and waited while he made her something to eat.

When he came out of the kitchen he handed her a sandwich. "Peanut butter and jelly, you need the protein," he stated and sat with one of his own.

She appreciated that he hadn't tried to give her meat. She wasn't even sure he knew she was vegetarian. It wasn't as if they'd ever shared a meal before and he certainly wasn't one. She knew werewolves needed meat to survive and that didn't bother her.

They ate in silence. She finished hers but he only ate half of his before setting the plate down. His stomach probably wasn't fully back to normal and a pang of guilt stabbed at her.

"I have your cat," she said, breaking the silence.

"Why?"

"I don't know, I kind of accidentally stole it when I first came to check on you. Then I just left it at my place figuring if you were out of it you might eat it or something. Is it even safe for you to own a cat?"

He grunted. "Yes, it is safe for me to own a cat."

She was doubtful.

"Are you really okay?" she asked quietly.

He looked up and met her gaze. His dark eyes were intense, and she almost wanted to shrink away from them. Her mind filled with images of him busting through her door, but also of how helpless he'd been the last few days. She couldn't decide which of those things were true. Was he a monster, or was he a lonely and helpless creature?

"Yes, Aurora, I am okay and I am going to continue to be okay," he finally said.

"I really am sorry about the cookies. I had no idea they would do that to you."

"I know."

She sighed and stood to clean up the plates. She took them to the kitchen and then went to the front door. "I'll leave you to rest. If you need anything, let me know. I wrote my number on a paper in the kitchen."

"I could literally yell if I needed you," he pointed out.

"What if I'm not home?"

He growled in response and she remembered that part of this had all started because he didn't want her going anywhere without him. Which reminded her why she'd come to discover him sick in the first place.

"Oh, I took a test, I'm really pregnant."

"I know."

"Yeah, well, I'm not a werewolf so I wanted the test."

He grunted. "I will want Peggy back," he said as she opened the door.

"Peggy?"

"My cat."

She didn't respond, just shut the door and hurried to her house. She was undecided if she could trust him with the cat.

CHAPTER THIRTEEN

Aurora slept most of the rest of the day and when she woke up it was to Claire knocking on her door.

"Did you kill him? Is that why you aren't answering my texts?" she demanded. "Do I need to help you create a new identity or bury a body?"

Aurora held the door open for her friend and laughed. "No, but I did nurse him back to health to ensure he didn't die and so that I wouldn't end up in prison for the rest of my life."

"Good plan, so he's okay?"

"Yeah, he finally woke up coherent this morning, but tired. It may be another day or two before he's fully recovered and I just slept most of the day away."

"Okay, so … did you two talk about how you're having a baby together?"

Aurora rolled her eyes. "We aren't having a baby *together.* I am having a baby, and it is both of ours—" she trailed off because the distinction was weak at best. "No, we didn't discuss anything."

"But you told him you took the test and things are official beyond his wolf's instincts?"

"I did, but he didn't need the extra confirmation like I did."

"Of course not, werewolves are all about instincts over science."

"Why do you know so much about werewolves?"

"I went to school in Oceanview, there were plenty of werewolves there."

Aurora had been raised on a small commune, missing out on a lot of the worldliness that her friend seemed to have gotten.

"Can I ask you something without you totally freaking out on me?"

"Probably not, but go ahead," Claire said eagerly.

"Werewolves are driven to find their mates and then stick with them forever, breed them full of babies and shit, right?"

"You make it sound so romantic," Claire teased.

Aurora rolled her eyes. "My *point* is, what about me? Is he going to have those feelings for me just because of the baby? Like we did it backwards and got the baby first but his wolf instincts are going to latch onto me now because of it?"

"Would you like him to?" Claire asked with a grin.

An image of Onyx's bare ass flashed in her mind and she had to shake herself before she could respond. It was better and worse than remembering the way he looked when he busted through her back door half formed. "Claire, this is serious."

She was grinning knowingly. "I don't think it works that way. I knew of at least one accidental pregnancy in my high school between werewolves and it didn't end with them getting married and being together forever. They took care of the kid well, got along okay as co-parents, but it didn't force any kind of bond. They both got married to other people after high school and had other kids."

Aurora nodded, she should be relieved. "That's good. I wouldn't want to be stuck with an infatuated werewolf neighbor."

"Of course not, especially one who makes you drool," Claire teased and leaned forward to mock wipe Aurora's chin.

"Oh shut up," Aurora snarled and threw a pillow at her friend.

The cat walked in then and jumped up on Aurora's lap.

"When did you get a cat?"

"It's Onyx's cat, her name is Peggy."

"A werewolf with a cat? That seems weird."

"Right? I brought her over here when he was sick because I didn't want him to eat her while he was delirious."

"Probably a good idea, she's too cute to be food."

Aurora handed the sweet cat to Claire and watched her friend give it kisses and coos. Did Onyx give the cat that kind of attention? She couldn't imagine him kissing and cuddling anything.

That was a lie, she could imagine him kissing and cuddling her, but she tried very hard not to.

"Woah girl, what's got you biting your lip?" Claire asked.

"Nothing. Want to walk down to the pond?" she asked, hoping to keep her friend from digging. There was a pond a mile down the road that made a nice walk and Aurora needed to clear her head. She was never good at keeping things from Claire when pressed. Usually it didn't matter because she didn't want to keep anything from Claire, but whatever she might be feeling for Onyx was too confusing to share just yet. It was probably just Florence Nightingale syndrome anyway, once he was well and back to his asshole self she'd forget how good he looked naked.

"Sure, we can pick some wildflowers."

Onyx watched the two women walk out of the house and down the road. They weren't going far on foot, he knew that, but he didn't like it. He was still feeling weak even though he'd napped and eaten some meat, and admitted he should probably rest some more. But he was feeling well enough to protect what was his.

The thought had him hesitating because he wasn't sure if he meant the baby or Aurora.

It didn't matter. He needed to keep a watch over them both at this point because they were a combined unit.

Onyx left the house and slipped into the woods. He knew where they were headed, he'd scented Aurora at the nearby pond many times. It seemed to be one of her favorite places to wander.

He didn't want to invade her privacy, or have to explain why he was following them, so he stayed as far back as he could and still see them. He couldn't hear what they were talking about, but he caught her laughter every once in a while, and he enjoyed it more than he should. It was obvious that Claire was a great friend to Aurora and he was glad she had that. He'd had that once, before he'd had to leave everything behind. Most days he was fine with it, but seeing them together now, knowing that Aurora would be sharing her thoughts and concerns with Claire about the baby, and likely him too, made him yearn for that closeness. What really caught him off guard was that he wanted that closeness with Aurora.

Fuck, he was a sad ass lonely werewolf. Maybe that's why he was feeling so possessive over Aurora and the baby. Maybe he just needed to go get laid, because obviously he wasn't going to go get a best friend or confidant out of nowhere.

As he watched, the two women gathered flowers and dipped their toes in the still cold water. Onyx swam in it year-round but he'd bet they only went in when it was peak summer hot.

They sat together on the shore for over an hour and talked. Knowing there was no danger in the area—he could smell everything in a five mile radius—he had no real excuse to keep watching the two. He slunk back home feeling like a complete loser. For the first time since he'd moved himself out here he questioned the wisdom of cutting himself off so completely. Werewolves generally stayed close to family or created a pack wherever they were. He'd avoided that, and he hadn't regretted it until now.

He couldn't do anything about the loneliness of no pack, but he could do something about physical loneliness. There was a place he had gone to a few times a year when he'd been super desperate for a meaningless connection and release. Maybe that's exactly what he needed now.

Three hours later he was parked outside the Full Moon bar. It was busy tonight, perfect for what he was going to do. Find an anonymous fuck. The bar was a large log building with space for some outdoor music and dancing on weekends tucked away outside of the city of Larkspring, but close enough that it drew a lot of werewolf traffic.

Customers were walking in and when the door opened he could see it was packed despite it being mid-week. Music and conversation could be heard and he knew without a doubt he'd find someone in that crowd willing to give him a moment of connection and relief.

So why was he still sitting in the parking lot?

He glanced down at his phone where he'd saved Aurora's phone number earlier that day. She'd told him to call her if he needed anything. The thought of telling her what he needed right now had his cock hardening. She would spit in his face if he told her he needed a good fuck.

He opened the door and stepped out of the truck then strode toward the bar with determination instead of the usual anticipation. A few vaguely familiar faces were among the crowd but most were nameless werewolves and that's what he liked. He went straight to the bar and ordered a beer.

The bartender was a thirty something man with a handlebar mustache and a tribal tattoo on his neck. Onyx knew his name was Jim and he was the son of the owner of this establishment.

"Been a while since the lone wolf was here," Jim commented with a raised eyebrow.

Onyx had never shared his name with this guy, or anyone else in the bar. "Don't need company very often," he said with a shrug. They both knew what he was here for.

"I thought maybe you finally went feral or figured out our species can't survive on our own and got yourself a pack."

Onyx just grunted, he wasn't interested in bartender therapy so he took his beer and walked to the edge of the room. He stood in shadow and leaned against the wall assessing the crowd, looking for something that piqued his interest.

He didn't want any blondes and no one slim and tall. He definitely wasn't interested in anyone wearing a sundress and sandals.

"Hey stranger, are you new around here?" A woman had sidled up to him. A voluptuous redhead in tight jeans and high heeled boots. Her tube-top was revealing everything and she in no way reminded him of Aurora. She was exactly what he'd been looking for when he came in here.

"Not interested," he snarled and she huffed before walking away and immediately approaching another man.

"Thought that's what you came here for," a waitress said as she gathered empty bottles from a nearby table. She must have worked here for a while if she recognized him and what he usually did when he showed up. He didn't recognize her, but that wasn't a surprise, he didn't *try* to remember anyone here.

"Usually," he agreed.

"So why is today different? Is Jim right, did you finally settle down? Find a mate and knock her up? Did the lone wolf become a family man?" she asked it with such doubt it made him bristle. As if he weren't capable of such a thing or didn't deserve to have all that she just described.

Maybe he didn't.

"Exactly," he said and put his half empty beer on her tray and walked out more twisted up than when he'd arrived.

The drive home wasn't long enough for him to settle his

thoughts and after he parked he stalked across his and Aurora's yards to knock on her door.

She opened it after long enough for him to realize she'd likely been in bed. It was late but he couldn't undo his knock so he didn't bother apologizing. She wore a thick pink robe and her hair was in two long braids. She clung to the robe like she wasn't wearing much underneath and he wanted to tear it off of her and see for himself. The thought kept him from speaking. He could only stare and wonder.

"Are you sick?" she snapped. "You better be dying to wake me up in the middle of the night." Her sleepy eyes ran up and down his body, likely noticing that he was dressed nicer than usual and not in stay-at-home sweats like she'd seen him last. She frowned and leaned forward, smelling him. His cheeks heated at the rush of adrenaline that the thought of her drawing his scent in spiked through his body. "Do you smell like a fucking bar?" she hissed.

Shame washed over him in a chilling wave. "I came for my cat," he gritted, completely chickening out on what his intention had been when coming here.

"Your cat, sure, that couldn't have waited until morning." She turned and walked into the other room. When she came back she was cradling Peggy.

"She likes you."

"Of course she likes me, she knows I'm not going to eat her."

"I don't eat cats," he defended.

"Sure." She handed him the cat and crossed her arms over her chest. His gaze was drawn down to where the robe was now slightly parted revealing the hint of sage green lace. "Is that all or can I go back to bed?"

"Litter box," he growled.

Aurora turned and got the litter box and shoved it at him. "Now is that all?"

No it wasn't all, he wanted to shout. He wanted to growl and intimidate her into stepping back so he could follow her inside. He wanted to peel that robe from her and see what the rest of that lace looked like on her delectable body. But he knew he couldn't do any of that so he grumbled, "Goodnight, Aurora." And he turned away.

Peggy started to purr in his arms soothingly. He wasn't a lonely werewolf, he had a cat.

CHAPTER FOURTEEN

Aurora slept in and woke up feeling great. She had lots of energy as she danced around the kitchen blasting music and making herself a protein-packed breakfast, because she knew how important protein was for growing a baby of any kind. She thought especially a half-werewolf one.

By the time she was eating it though, her energy had turned itself into worry and she pulled out her laptop to do a little research. Certainly she wasn't the first human woman to have a werewolf baby and she needed to know what to expect. She also needed to make a prenatal appointment with a doctor who might have experience

The internet search was less helpful and more terrifying. Stories that she was certain had to be made up, she hoped they were made up. Like children born to a regular married human couple but it coming out covered in fur with claws and a penchant for raw meat.

Her stomach turned at the thought of feeding her newborn raw steak instead of a bottle.

After a little more digging she got past the clickbait stories and found an article about a woman in England who had dated and fallen in love with a werewolf. They hadn't thought it possible, but she ended up pregnant and their child had come out healthy. They had kept out of the press and lived in a secluded area where they thought they could give the child a good chance to grow up without being a science project for the world to watch. So unfortunately there wasn't much for her to know, other than the child apparently had come out alright and was still alive five years later.

That was promising.

She sighed and switched to searching for OB-GYNs in her area that saw both human and werewolf clients. The closest one was in Larkspring. Not ideal, but she'd drive the extra time for a doctor who knew what she was doing. Plus they had a birthing clinic they partnered with that was closer to Greensferry.

Aurora filled out the online application for an appointment as a new client then shut the laptop feeling accomplished.

She wasn't sure how much involvement she wanted to offer Onyx, but she had a feeling he'd want to do some things with her. Especially since he didn't want her going anywhere without him. She'd thought she would drag Claire to her prenatal appointments with her and have her mother go to birthing classes but now she wondered if Onyx should be doing those things with her. It was going to be weird to involve him, and what would they tell people if asked? *Oh he's just a sperm donor, literally, but hey we're neighbors so he's going to attend the birth and be a father...* Ugh, it was too much.

She didn't have answers so she distracted herself by calling her father.

"Hey sweetie, is your neighbor hanging in there?"

"He is. I stayed with him until it passed."

She could practically hear her father frowning on the other side of the line. "You shouldn't be around a sick and delirious werewolf, it's dangerous."

"He never once was aggressive towards me. He was pretty helpless actually." A term she never imagined applying to her neighbor.

"Okay, well I'm glad he's better and I am guessing you'll think twice before giving someone poisoned cookies again."

"I will definitely think about it longer next time," she agreed with a laugh. "Can you ask Jason if he knows of any human and werewolf couples with kids. I tried to look online but didn't come up with much."

"Will do. I'll be seeing him for a shift tonight."

"Thanks Dad."

After that she decided to work in her garden. She already needed to do some weeding around her sprouting veggies. She changed into her gardening clothes, a pair of cotton shorts with little pineapples all over them and a tight pink tank top. They were old and already stained and perfect for working in the dirt. She pulled her hair up into a bun and wrapped a scarf around it to keep at least most of the dust out of it. She didn't bother with shoes, she loved the feeling of getting her toes into the earth.

An hour later she was sweaty and dirty and feeling at peace. Footsteps interrupted that and she knew exactly who they belonged to.

"Hey Onyx," she said when he stopped at her side. She looked up at him with a half smile. He was looking a little more clean than usual, as if he hadn't just come from working with wood in his driveway. She'd known that's exactly what he'd been doing, she had heard it when she started her own outdoor project, but he must have stopped and cleaned up before approaching her. Something about that made her want to tease him but she held back.

He eyed her with a frown, his eyes seeming to linger on her dirty feet. "Do you need to go to town today?"

She sighed heavily and stood. "Do I look like I'm about to head to town?" she asked.

"No, but I've seen you clean up and leave in a hurry before."

"Stalker," she said with a laugh. He glared. "I wasn't planning on it, why? Do you need me to pick up some cat food? Or puppy chow?" she couldn't help adding with a wicked grin.

Onyx held his features still, not allowing any hint at what he was feeling. "I would go in if you needed to go in."

"Of course you would, and if I tried to go without you, you'd probably follow me or slash my tires when I returned."

His eyes widened. "I would never do something like that. It would be dangerous for you to be out here without a means of getting to town in an emergency."

She noticed he didn't mention he wouldn't chase her to town if she tried to go without him.

She gritted her teeth and tried to keep herself centered. She knew he was a different species and she knew that his instincts were not the same as hers. She couldn't treat him like an asshole human because he wasn't a human, he was an asshole wolf.

"I will probably go to town in a day or two. I'm waiting to hear back about a doctor appointment actually, so I might even be going into Larkspring in the next week."

"Why do you need to see the doctor? What's wrong?" he asked, his voice high with panic. His eyes went to her stomach then flew back up to meet hers.

"I'm pregnant," she said flatly. "Or did you forget?"

"Oh, right. I suppose you would need to go for that. Just to make sure things are where they should be?"

"Yep, don't want the damn thing to attach to my lungs," she said with an eye roll. Did this guy not understand anything about pregnancy?

He shook his head, obviously knowing he was talking nonsense. "Well, I, uh, I would appreciate if you let me know when you plan to do that and I will go along."

"To keep creeps away? Or to hear the heartbeat?" she asked,

truly curious about what his ideas about involvement with the pregnancy were.

He took a step back and his shoulders rose as if he were steadying himself with a deep breath. "I would like to be there as much as you'd allow. I know this isn't what you had planned, but my instincts are undeniably protective of the child even now."

It bothered her that he specified the baby over her, even though she knew she shouldn't care. This wasn't a relationship. She plastered a smile on her face. "Sure, I'll let you know and you can tag along."

He nodded and she waited for him to turn and walk away. He shifted on his feet and she was pretty sure she heard a slight rumble in his chest. Whatever he was working himself up to say was important and it started to make her nervous.

"Is there something else, Onyx?"

"Please don't schedule anything or leave your house on the full moon," he said and she saw a vulnerability in him that tugged at her.

"Okay," she agreed.

That seemed to please him and he gave her a small smile before turning and walking away.

"Do you want to come over for dinner and you can fill out some of the paperwork?" she called to his back, not sure what had provoked her mouth to spill out the offer. Did she really want him in her house, eating her food? Did she really need him to fill out paperwork now rather than in the office at some point?

She wasn't sure what the answer was, but something was tight in her stomach and she wanted to offer him an olive branch. If he could be vulnerable with her, she could be welcoming to him.

He turned to her, not hiding the surprise on his face. "That would be fine, but I won't let you cook for me, I'll make dinner and bring it over."

She wasn't sure if that was a reference to her poisoning him or not so she just nodded. "I'm vegetarian."

"I know," he said and turned to walk away.

"I'll make dessert," she called to his back.

His shoulders stiffened but he didn't respond.

Onyx was happy as he walked to Aurora's house with dinner in his hands. He hadn't dressed up necessarily, but he had made an effort to look nice. He was freshly showered and wearing black shorts with no holes and a black T-shirt rather than his usual button up plaid work-shirt. He'd even cleaned under his fingernails and there was no sawdust in his hair, which he'd brushed and left loose around his shoulders. Usually he tied it up because although he loved that it was as long as he wanted with no one telling him to cut it, it always got in the way of his work. He was a little nervous. Had Aurora ever seen him like this? What if she didn't like it?

And why did he care so much if she did?

She had invited him into her home and she was allowing him to feed her. She also hadn't balked at the idea of him attending the doctor's appointment with her. He really hadn't expected that but if this was going to work, he needed her to see him as a partner. Which is what had pushed him to approach her in the yard. He'd wanted to establish a friendly rapport, but he'd expected it to be harder. He thought back to every time they'd ever interacted and grimaced as he realized that she wasn't the instigator most of the time. She reacted and repaid whatever he'd put out there and from the very first meeting he'd put out there that he wasn't interested in being friendly. He was lucky that she wasn't holding that against him now.

Aurora opened the door before Onyx had to figure out how to knock with his hands full and she was smiling in welcome.

She is absolutely beautiful.

The thought came from his wolf, but he couldn't deny it was

true. She was stunning as she stood there in a long white skirt and purple tank top. Her hair was braided and her face was clean of makeup making her green eyes and freckles stand out. She was exactly what he would want in a mate welcoming him back to his den at night. And him, carrying food for her and their child made his chest swell with a pride he didn't know he could feel.

This was every werewolf's dream.

Too bad it wasn't what it appeared to be. She wouldn't lay down next to him tonight and she wouldn't share kisses or touches with him. She wasn't his, even if she was having his child.

"What did you make? It smells amazing." She asked as she led the way to the kitchen where the table was set for two.

"Roast vegetables and a lentil loaf."

"I think my stomach just growled," she laughed.

The satisfaction he got from her anticipation to eat the food he'd provided was something he'd never experienced in his life. He didn't know what to say to her that wasn't animalistic and awkwardly possessive, so he just set the food down on the table. He hadn't even known what a lentil loaf was before this afternoon but thank the gods for internet. He still wasn't sure it was edible, but she looked impressed so he hoped it was.

"I have water, herbal iced tea, or lemonade. Sorry, nothing stronger."

"Tea is good."

She poured two glasses and they sat at the table. When she pulled the lid off of the dish she groaned and his shorts tightened.

"My mouth is watering, Onyx, I had no idea you were such an amazing cook."

He didn't trust his voice with the image of her watering mouth in his head, so he just grunted and started to dish out the food. He put a healthy portion of the loaf on her plate and some veggies before serving himself.

"How did you know that I was a vegetarian?"

"I can smell your cooking, and never once has it been meat," he said, slightly embarrassed to admit he'd paid attention. She'd already called him a stalker once today, this was just further proof that he'd paid way more attention to her than he'd like to admit.

"Oh, yeah that makes sense," she said and speared a piece of loaf with her fork.

His eyes were glued to her as she brought the bite to her mouth. His hands gripped his own cutlery with white knuckles in an attempt at keeping himself in control when all he wanted to do was throw the table away from them and close the distance to her.

She opened her plump pink lips and put the food that *he'd* cooked into her mouth. Her eyes closed as she tasted it and her whole body seemed to slump with a relaxed moan as she began to chew.

The sound of cracking porcelain broke the spell and Aurora's eyes popped open. They both stared down at his now broken plate. His fork had gone right through the damn thing.

"Sorry," he said.

She burst out laughing. "Oh my god, you're a beast, Onyx."

He didn't appreciate the accusation, but she seemed amused, so he supposed it wasn't derogatory.

"I'm sorry," he reiterated and hurried to sweep the entire mess into a garbage can she'd dragged over.

"Don't worry about it. I bought them at a secondhand store. It's not like they were precious." She grabbed a clean plate out of the cabinet and put it on the table in front of him. She didn't move away so he looked up at her smiling face. "Besides, it's not the first thing in my house you've broken."

"I'll try not to make it a habit," he said dryly but he didn't stop the smile that stretched his lips.

She looked a little shocked by his humor as she finally moved away from him and back to her seat. He served himself another portion as she began eating again.

The rest of the meal passed without incident but he struggled to keep his eyes off her mouth and his mind off the noises of enjoyment she was making. His body didn't get the memo to even try however, because for the first time since he was over the age of fifteen, he ate an entire meal with a hard on.

CHAPTER FIFTEEN

Aurora brought out her laptop as Onyx cleared the table and started loading the dishwasher. Dinner had been surprisingly pleasant, and delicious. He'd even joked, that had really caught her off guard. It was far more surprising than him breaking a plate had been. He was also dressed up for her and his hair, dear lord his hair! She'd never seen it loose like that except when he had been sick and sweaty. It was beautiful; long and dark and smooth. She could tell it was healthy, obviously he took good care of it. That surprised her as much as the fact that he had a cat and cooked a great lentil loaf. She'd thought she knew everything she cared to know about her grumpy werewolf neighbor, but maybe there was more to him. And maybe she wanted to discover it all.

"Do you have work to do?" he asked, nodding toward her computer.

"No, I'm not doing any kind of summer school, online or otherwise. I was actually thinking it might make things go faster if we got some of this father information filled out ahead of time."

"For the doctor?"

"Yeah, I don't have an appointment set yet, but I'm sure that will come soon and since you're here I figure why not."

"Okay," he agreed without looking at her.

"Full name?"

"Onyx Timothy West."

"Cute," she commented and his shoulder's stiffened. She kept the rest of her comments to herself as she asked for other bits of information.

His genetic history was as bland as her own, no predispositions to anything and no history of congenital birth defects in his family.

"And no other children," she said with a laugh as if it were obvious.

"No," he growled in a way that told her there was a whole lot more to that answer, but he was obviously not in a mood to share.

Like that had ever stopped her before.

"Did you ever plan to have kids?"

"No."

"Is that why you donated sperm? So that your superior genetics could be out there without you being a parent?"

"No."

She sighed then changed tactics.

"Werewolves usually have large families, so how many siblings did you grow up with?"

He slammed the dishwasher shut. "Let me know when your appointment is," he snarled and left the house.

"Grumpy," she commented and shut her laptop. "I hope that's not genetic."

Aurora spent the next week trying not to obsess about the way Onyx's face had softened into a smile at dinner. It helped that every time she saw him after that he was wearing his usual blank face or scowling. Maybe she'd never see that smile again. Something about that made her sad.

Her father called back to report that James didn't know any human and werewolf couples. She asked her mother the same thing and got the same answer. Aurora didn't like the idea that she was doing something so new and different. She made some extra offerings to the Moon Goddess who was apparently the one who had done this to her, hoping that it would guarantee a healthy child as a result.

She took one trip to town with Onyx for groceries and it went surprisingly well. She wasn't sure she'd call it pleasant, but it at least wasn't cut short. She talked in the car and he sat there listening to her, but he didn't contribute much to the conversation. Luckily she was a teacher and so she was very used to talking without a guarantee anyone was listening. When they got to the store he seemed to pay very careful attention to everything she was buying.

"Don't you need things too?" she asked when they were halfway through and he hadn't put anything in his own cart.

"Oh," he said as if he were just then realizing that he hadn't picked out anything. He moved off to get his own things which she noticed included many items that were in her cart too. She also noticed that the meat he'd picked out was hidden under vegetables and when they checked out he went to a different lane than her. Was he embarrassed about his need for meat?

"Werewolves have different anatomy than humans," Aurora said as they drove home.

He gave her a look that said he thought that might be the dumbest thing he'd ever heard.

Aurora laughed. "I guess what I'm trying to say is that I understand you need meat. I don't eat it, but I understand that you need to, I don't judge you for that."

"What will you do if the child needs meat?" he asked.

Aurora pursed her lips and took a deep breath through her

nose. She'd thought about that, a lot. "I will see what the pediatrician recommends of course. I want to provide the best for the child. I had planned to raise it vegetarian until it was old enough to make its own choices. It's the same way my parents raised me. But I guess that might not work, depending on the child's specific genetic needs."

He seemed satisfied with that answer. "I like vegetables, I am just not completely satisfied with them."

"Like I said, I understand."

"If the child needs meat, I can provide that for it."

"Thank you."

"Peggy has to have meat as well."

"Yes, cats need meat."

"I prefer to hunt for my own meat when I can and I only kill what I eat, I don't waste life."

Aurora felt like they were having two different conversations.

"I am not sure I can be more clear, Onyx. I am not judging your dietary needs."

He looked at her quizzically, as if he didn't believe she wasn't judging him. Maybe they'd spent so much time at odds that he wasn't able to believe her acceptance of this rather large difference in their lifestyles.

"I am sure there are a lot of things we do differently," she said. "I have lots of friends and I go to work around people. I talk all day. You … like to be alone. I get that. I don't think I've ever seen you out exercising for fun, you are just naturally fit. I like to go on walks and ride my bike to the pond and swim to keep in shape."

"You have family that cares for you, I have Peggy," he added and her heart dropped even though she was sure he hadn't said it for sympathy. He'd stated it like just another random fact about them both, but it made her hurt for him.

"Hey, I'm growing you a family member right now," she joked.

His eyes went to her flat belly and he seemed about to say

something but then turned to stare out his window. They rode home the rest of the way in silence aside from the radio.

Onyx carried in her groceries before taking his own into his house. She'd tried to argue that she didn't need his help, but his look had silenced her. Sometimes she wasn't completely irritating. Sometimes she said or did something so perfect it destroyed him in a way her anger and revenge schemes never could.

She was growing him a family member. Those words had torn through him so sharply he didn't think he'd ever recover. She was doing so much more than that though. She was *becoming* his pack. She and the baby would be everything he needed or wanted and it terrified him that she didn't realize it. Did she think that all he would want was the baby? Of course she did, why wouldn't she? He hadn't given her any reason to think otherwise because he didn't want to see her laugh in his face. He couldn't bear the thought of her denying him any part of herself.

So he let her believe what she would, because the alternative was too scary.

He paused on his porch, a package had been delivered on his doorstep while they'd been out. He picked it up wondering why he'd even bothered ordering the damn thing. He threw it unopened on the kitchen table. Maybe he'd just send it back. It wasn't as if he'd be needing to cook for her very often. Ordering a vegetarian cookbook had been a stupid and impulsive thing for him to do. He could always give it to her as a gift, but she probably knew more than the book.

Onyx unloaded the groceries, his bags were full of things he'd seen her grab that he would have never bought for himself. Probably another stupid move. Why was he trying to learn what she liked?

He looked back at the package.

Maybe he'd be cooking vegetarian meals for his child. The thought brought a smile to his face. What if it was a delicate little human like her and he'd be feeding it tiny cucumber sandwiches and fresh pressed juice. The idea would terrify him more if he hadn't managed to keep Peggy alive for three years.

He opened the package and sat to read through the cookbook. Whether he was cooking for Aurora or not, it would make sense to learn how to make vegetarian meals that provided the right nutrition and tasted good.

CHAPTER SIXTEEN

On the morning of the full moon Aurora was sitting outside as she often did, enjoying a cup of coffee. Onyx approached her with a look somewhere between frantic and outraged.

"Good morning, Onyx," she said carefully. Perhaps she should have changed her plans because it was the full moon tonight, but fuck him if he thought she was going to tiptoe around his hormonal cycle. It hadn't been an issue in the past, why would it be now?

"It's a full moon tonight."

"Yep."

"Are you planning to leave the house today or tonight?"

"Nope."

"Good." He turned to leave.

She stood, not willing to put up with his shit. "Hey, if you don't give me more than that then I'm taking my ass to town and maybe I'll stay all night."

He turned quickly and stalked back, his eyes flashing yellow. "It's not a good day to mess with me, Aurora."

"You don't get to order me around Onyx. So start talking." She wasn't sure where her confidence came from, but she wasn't afraid of him. Not even when he bared his teeth slightly.

"I will want to keep you safe," he said as if every word was being forced out of his mouth.

"Safe?"

"I will need to know where you are, especially tonight."

"And if I wasn't here?"

He walked up the steps and moved until he was towering over her. She refused to lean away. "I'd hunt you down," he snarled.

It didn't feel like a threat, it felt like the most erotic promise she'd ever heard. Aurora had to swallow to get the next question out. "And then what would you do?"

"I'd devour you," he said and his eyes skimmed down her body then back up to meet her gaze. "Until you screamed my name."

"Jesus," she breathed.

He straightened and walked away, leaving her on fire.

"Fucking Christ, I think I just came." A shiver ran through her body as she watched him cross to his house and go inside.

She turned on slightly shaking legs and went straight to her bedroom where she pulled out her vibrator. She'd never been so turned on in her life and that included every sexual interaction she'd ever had with a boyfriend.

It didn't take her long to get herself to climax, and when she did she covered her face with a pillow because she knew the name on her lips wasn't going to stay inside.

That wasn't what Onyx had meant to do. He only wanted to ascertain her plans for the day and request she stay home so he could do his usual full moon thing. He had wanted to let her know he'd likely be drawn closer to her house than usual so maybe she could not turn the sprinklers on him this time.

But as soon as he was close to her he'd wanted to grab her and take her to the bedroom. All he could think about was sinking his cock into her heat. He'd been hard and ready, and his blood was pumping like crazy while his wolf howled encouragement in his mind. He hadn't been able to handle her teasing. If she actually left their properties today he wasn't lying about what he'd do. He would hunt her down wherever she was, with one goal in mind.

Claiming her and marking her as his own.

He walked straight to his bathroom and leaned over the sink. He shoved a hand down his pants because if he didn't relieve some of this pressure he was going to explode. This need had been building all week and he'd masturbated daily to her image, but this was the first time he didn't think it would be enough.

And he was right because after he groaned his release he felt the need starting over. Now he understood why mated wolves spent the first year of full moons alone. If this was the type of desire they were dealing with he couldn't imagine them wanting to be around their pack, or their pack wanting to be around them.

But Aurora wasn't his mate. She was just the mother of his child and the neighbor who was too much sunshine for his liking. His wolf wanted to argue but he shut it down, washed himself off, then went outside to lose himself in his work even though his cock was still half hard.

It was a good enough distraction until the sun started to set.

On a normal full moon night he'd eat a large dinner then head out to the woods behind his house and shift. Tonight he was far too anxious for that. He didn't eat and he didn't wait until the evening was dark.

He shifted at sunset, stomach empty and began a slow pace around Aurora's house. He couldn't convince his wolf to do anything else. Her smell was wonderful and he wanted to roll around in it. He wanted to lap it up and he wanted to press his nose to her skin to inhale it direct from its source.

Fuck he wanted her.

"Are you going to be doing this all night?"

Her voice called to him from her back door. He'd been so distracted fantasizing about her that he hadn't noticed her open it.

He stopped and sat, staring at her out of his wolf eyes. He couldn't respond, but she knew that. She was wearing sweats and a loose T-shirt, lounge clothes that he knew she liked to put on whenever the weather was cool. He'd seen her sit on her front porch in these clothes and read a book when the rain fell on her days off. He had always liked it. It was so different than her usual bright outfits that it made him feel like he was glimpsing a secret other part of her that no one else knew about. He wanted to know all of her parts and he wanted some of them to be only for him.

"I'll take that as a yes. Is this all about me being pregnant? You can't go far because you want to protect the baby?"

That wasn't completely correct, but he wouldn't have told her the whole truth if he could.

"It's going to rain. The news says lightning too and it sounds like it might be a bad one. There's no tree cover on the track you're wearing in my lawn."

He didn't care. His dark fur was thick. He got up and started to walk again. He would feel bad if he wore a path in her grass, but he could always offer to re-seed it for her. By the time he got back to the rear of the house she was back inside and the first drops of rain were starting to fall.

He continued on his path as the rain pounded and the lightning and thunder started in the distance. Normally this weather would have him resting under the cover of trees, but his comfort wasn't as important as her safety so he wouldn't hide. After about an hour and no end in sight for the storm, she opened the back door again.

"Get in the house, Onyx. If you get struck by lightning I'll feel guilty and that's probably bad for the baby."

He didn't think it was a good idea, but it was exactly what he wanted so he bounded up the steps and crowded her inside. He stopped there, unsure because he didn't want to shake off the water in her kitchen so he stood dripping on her floor.

"I'll get a towel," she said.

Her smell was even better in this form and his wolf was so happy to be in her home it started to shiver. When she came back with a towel she tsked and started to rub him down.

"I told you it was too cold and wet to be out there, even for a furry guy," she chastised.

She was wrong, but he would rather be in here with her than anywhere else.

She stood when she was satisfied that he was dry and then looked at him as if she wasn't sure what the next step was. "I was just watching a movie, want to join me?"

Fuck yeah, he did. He walked to the living room and sat on the floor.

"Okay, I think I like you in this form better," she said with a laugh and sat back on the couch where she had obviously been curled up. She had a blanket and a bowl of popcorn set out. She pressed play on the movie and he lay content in a way he usually only was after hunting in this form. Right now he didn't want to be anywhere else in the world.

Eventually her breathing evened out and he knew she'd fallen asleep. He moved closer to her and laid down. He let his own eyes slide shut and drifted into contented sleep knowing his pack was safe and near him.

Onyx woke up with the first rays of sunshine and stretched, confused by why he felt carpet under him instead of grass. Then the scents of her filled him with desire and he remembered where he was. Now fully human again, his cock swelled embarrassingly. He moved as slow as possible, hoping not to wake and terrify Aurora with the sight of a naked man in her living room. Thankfully he could tell by the sound of her breathing that she was still asleep. He wished he could stay and stare at her but if she woke up he'd feel like a total creep. So he quickly filled his mind with the image of her sleeping contentedly near him then turned to leave.

Unfortunately he stepped on the remote and the sounds of a morning show filled the room. Aurora bolted upright and she let out a little scream. He turned to face her and apologize, of course that just presented her at eye level with his engorged cock and it was all she seemed to be able to focus on. Her green eyes sparkled and her mouth dropped open as she took him in.

Having her eyes on him like that was too much. He groaned and grasped himself which snapped her out of her shock and she turned and buried her face in the couch.

"Oh god, what the hell are you doing? You should leave I think," she said, her voice muffled in the pillow.

"Yeah," he grunted, still gripping his cock. He forced himself to turn away from her and leave the house.

And just like the morning before, he went straight to his bathroom to stroke his cock because of her.

CHAPTER SEVENTEEN

"What do you mean he slept on your floor naked," Claire demanded as they sat together on Aurora's front porch.

Aurora had called Claire over for an emergency chat and she'd shown up with doughnuts and an eager ear.

"I think they shift in their sleep after the full moon. I don't think he would have intentionally just been there naked in front of me. I'm pretty sure he was trying to sneak out when I woke up."

"With morning wood?" Claire asked while wiggling her eyebrows.

Aurora hadn't elaborated on that but she couldn't stop thinking about it. His cock had been huge and uncut and intriguing. And the way he'd grasped it when she looked, as if he was enjoying her stare, not trying to hide his nakedness from her. She was sure she'd never get the vision out of her mind, or the feeling of desire that had spiked through her even as she told him to leave.

"Doesn't every guy have morning wood?" Aurora reasoned.

Claire shrugged agreement. "And why did you invite him in last night? He's a fur-covered wolf, he can handle the rain."

"I know, but the lightning was getting close and he wouldn't go under the tree cover. He just kept circling my damn house like an idiot."

"Or like a predator circling its prey," she teased and giggled.

"He told me he would hunt me down and devour me if I left the house yesterday," Aurora admitted with a giggle.

"Oh my god, you're living my dream. Please tell me it's beautiful."

Aurora knew her friend wasn't talking about the man's abs.

"It was impressive." So impressive she hadn't wanted to look away from it.

Claire squealed and kicked her feet. "You have got to jump on that thing. He might not be so into you when the baby comes out, you need to take advantage."

"That's exactly what I'm afraid of," she sighed. "The man despises me for years and suddenly he's down to fuck. I am not interested in being the vessel for his breeding kink."

"Too late," Claire said and pointed at Aurora's stomach. "The man already bred you. You just missed out on the good part so why not go back and get it?"

Aurora hated to admit she wanted to do exactly that, but she knew she shouldn't.

Two weeks later Aurora was sitting in her car with Onyx headed to their first doctor's appointment. They'd spent the last two weeks awkwardly avoiding each other and she'd even had groceries delivered so she didn't have to deal with going to town with him. That hadn't turned out well because when Onyx had spotted the young man parking in front of her house he'd come running to investigate. He'd snapped and snarled at the poor delivery boy as if he were an armed intruder. Aurora had turned the hose on Onyx then ordered him to carry the groceries inside. Onyx had grumbled an apology to the boy and tipped him.

"Why did you pick a doctor that's an hour away?" he grumbled.

"Because they have experience with human and werewolf pregnancies and they are well recommended."

"What are you going to do, drive an hour in labor to have the baby? You should pick someone in town."

Aurora gripped the steering wheel and gritted her teeth. "Actually, they deliver at the rural hospital and that's only twenty minutes from us. This is just their main office."

"So the *doctor* is going to drive forty minutes when you're in labor just to deliver the baby for you?"

Aurora had to take a deep breath and settle her nerves. She was going to have some kind of insane blood pressure when they got there if Onyx kept this shit up. "An on-call doctor is available at the rural hospital at all times."

"So we are going to see a doctor today who may not even deliver the baby?"

"Yes," she snapped. It was going to be a long day.

The rest of the drive held very little conversation but Onyx did pump her gas for her and even washed her windshield, both of which she appreciated. She hadn't had this kind of princess treatment in a long time. Trent had stopped doing things like this for her after the first time she'd slept with him. That had probably been a red flag she should have heeded.

When she parked in front of the medical office building that held Morgan and Faller OB-GYN, she felt her gut tighten. She turned off the car and just stared for a minute.

Onyx watched her with a frown. "What's wrong, is this the right place?"

Aurora took a deep breath. "Yeah, it's the right place." She got out of the car, not wanting to explain to him that she was nervous and excited. And mostly she was unsure that she wanted to share this moment with him. It wasn't fair to put that on him, he was just as surprised and stuck in this as she was. Well, no, he was more surprised than her seeing as she'd literally paid to be in this position, just not with him.

She hurried out of the car before she could wallow in her nerves any longer. She smoothed out her knee-length skirt as she waited for Onyx to join her. He was wearing clean jeans and a T-shirt, his hair up in its usual bun. She'd decided that she preferred it down, particularly when he was naked.

No, it was not the time to be remembering how he'd looked standing in her living room.

"Ready?" he asked when she didn't start moving.

"Are you?"

"I am," he said with a surprising amount of confidence.

"Let's go see about this baby," she said with a smile.

Onyx walked close to her as they crossed the lot then held the door for her. The waiting room was busy, she supposed that was a good sign. There was a very friendly looking woman behind a large desk who greeted them as they approached.

"We are new," Aurora said nervously. "Aurora Port, I have an appointment."

"Great, I have you in, a nurse will call you back shortly."

Aurora led Onyx to a seat and he sat next to her. She picked up a parenting magazine on the nearby table but he just sat looking incredibly uncomfortable.

"This place sees werewolves?"

Aurora looked around the room realizing that he must not smell any other werewolves among the waiting patients. You couldn't always tell just by looking but she assumed he would know.

"They do, they take everything according to their website. The doctor we're seeing for most of the appointments is Dr. Shayla, she's a werewolf. Which I thought might be nice."

"Is she Morgan or Faller?" he asked.

"Actually she's neither. It's Dr. Shayla Blithe."

Onyx looked stricken but before she could ask what was the

matter, the nurse was calling them back. Aurora stood but Onyx seemed frozen.

Aurora touched his shoulder and he jumped and looked up at her with yellowed eyes.

"Do you want to wait out here?" Maybe he'd overestimated his ability to do this with her, maybe it was all becoming too real for him. She'd understand if he wanted to sit this out. After all she didn't need him with her, but she was willing to let him be there if he wanted to be, no pressure.

He shook his head and stood, not looking as calm as before. He followed her, silent and glowering. She stopped at the scale so she could be weighed, then they were showed to an exam room where her blood pressure was taken. The nurse asked her a few questions about the paperwork and how she was feeling. All of it she barely remembered because she couldn't stop watching Onyx who looked like he was about to have a panic attack. Even the nurse kept glancing his way warily.

"You'll need to strip from the waist down. The doctor will be right in." The nurse left the room as fast as she could.

"Can you wait outside while I change?"

"No."

Something told Aurora she shouldn't push him while he was going through whatever this was. "Then at least turn around. You aren't getting a free peep show even if I am pregnant with your child."

He grunted but obeyed, turning to stare at the wall. His shoulders were stiff and his arms were crossed. He looked like he was waiting for torture rather than a sonogram of his child. She undressed as fast as she could manage and hopped up on the table, covering her lower half with the paper blanket.

"Okay, you can turn around," she said, trying to keep her voice relaxed but she was a ball of nerves. Good thing the nurse had already taken her blood pressure.

. . .

Onyx was freaking out.

What were the chances that it was a different Shayla Blithe? What were the chances it wasn't and she didn't remember him? What were the chances that his past and present were about to crash together?

He knew he wasn't hiding his stress when he turned around and met Aurora's gaze. She looked even more nervous than before.

He cursed himself and stepped toward her. He needed to do everything possible to keep her calm and happy. It was best for the baby, he knew that much. He gave her a weak smile and a stupid excuse about hating doctors' offices.

She seemed to accept that and relaxed but then there was a knock on the door and in walked his past.

"Jesus fucking Christ, it really is you," Shayla said as she walked in, her eyes glued to Onyx.

"What's going on?" Aurora asked from the bed, her voice shaky.

Onyx couldn't look away from Shayla, there was a challenge in her eyes that his wolf didn't want to shy away from. "It's me," he agreed.

"Do you two know each other?" Aurora tried again weakly.

Shayla grunted and looked at Aurora for the first time. She closed the door behind her and walked closer to the table where Aurora was laying half naked and vulnerable.

Onyx hated it. Every instinct he had was yelling at him to grab Aurora and run, to tuck her away where she'd be safe.

"Hey, I'm Dr. Blithe, Shayla is fine. I don't mind anyone whose privates I'm up close and personal with using my first name," she joked. "And yes, I know this guy. Better question is, how do you know him? Is he really the father of this baby?"

"Yes," Aurora said sounding unsure.

Onyx was thankful she wasn't launching into the details of why and how they were having a child together.

"Onyx and I grew up together. He was supposed to marry my best friend, Rebecca who was knocked up."

"Not by me," Onyx growled.

"No, but by your dead brother and your father wanted you to do the right thing, she was pack, Onyx."

"Was it even his?" Onyx snarled.

"Yes, it was," Shayla said and met his gaze with a challenge that he knew meant she was telling the truth.

A blast of shock rocked his body but he refused to back down.

"You have a niece," she added, more calm now.

"That doesn't mean I should have married her," he snarled.

"No, Rebecca was best off left to suffer pregnancy and parenting alone. That's exactly how you're supposed to treat pack."

"Marrying someone who you don't love is torture for everyone, you know that. My father was probably happy to help her out anyway. His favorite son's child would be precious to him and like you said, she was pack."

"Yes, your father knew how to take responsibility for those under his care," she challenged.

Onyx had no response. He just bared his teeth at the woman who bared hers back.

"Do I need to pick a different doctor?" Aurora asked.

Shayla turned to her and shrugged. "Up to you. I'm a professional and I don't shirk my duties," she said, snapping the last at Onyx.

"Neither do I," Onyx snarled. "When they *are* mine."

Aurora sat up, clutching the paper blanket to her. "We should get a new doctor I think."

"Fine with me," Shayla said and walked out the door shooting one last look at Onyx. "I can't wait to tell Rebecca and Glen that I saw you."

Glen was Shayla's brother and had been Onyx's best friend. The most regrettable person who he'd disappeared on all those years ago. He was afraid of what Glen would think of him now, how disappointed he'd be in the choices Onyx had made back then. Would Glen think him as selfish as his sister obviously did?

As soon as the door closed he turned to Aurora who looked like she was about to launch into a litany of questions.

"Please get dressed, we need to leave. Choose any other doctor's office, please. I will drive you all the way to Oceanview if needed, but you can't be seen by anyone here. Not if there's a chance Shayla could deliver the baby."

Aurora clamped her lips shut and she didn't look happy about it, but she nodded in agreement.

"Thank you," he whispered and spun around to give her privacy.

Onyx kept as close to her as he could as she explained to the front desk that she wouldn't be a patient there and then he ushered her quickly to the car. As soon as he was seated, he growled at her to drive but she just crossed her arms and looked at him with a raised eyebrow in question.

"I swear I will tell you everything. Can we just get away from this place?" As if it would matter, the damage was already done.

"Fine," she said and started the car.

CHAPTER EIGHTEEN

When they were a mile down the road Onyx started to talk.

"Rebecca's family became a part of my father's pack when I was a child. Her family wasn't very well off, her dad was an alcoholic and her mom had died birthing her fifth child. Rebecca was somewhere in the middle of the litter, I can't remember exactly. My family was not like that. I was the second born of six and my parents both came from wealthy families. We had a lot, probably too much. Though one thing we had in common with Rebecca's family was that my mother also died in childbirth with our last sibling, so it bonded our families. I think that's why my father took them into our pack and even gave them a home on the edge of our property. My dad gave their father work here and there around the property and we were told to support the children like siblings, that is what it means to be pack, it's an extension of family. My father was big on responsibility and doing what was expected. I'm sure it came from the way he was raised, I never met my grandparents because they'd passed but it sounded like they were controlling and hadn't given my father much choice in what he would do with his own life. My big brother, Tanner, started dating Rebecca when they were both eighteen even though my father didn't see the family as marriageable. He'd been clear about it to us in private. I think my dad ignored their young love because my brother continued to do everything else my father instructed him to do. Tanner was being groomed to take over for my father as CEO of his company and would eventually be in charge of the pack too. Rebecca's dad didn't seem to care about anything his kids did, I think he was just happy Rebecca was dating someone wealthy."

"They were on and off for a couple of years. Despite the fact that Tanner was sneaking out every night to go meet with her and party, he still managed to be doing well in college and learning at my father's side. He was going somewhere, he was so smart and driven, he saw his whole life playing out ahead of him and he liked it. He wanted what my father had, I could tell. I was thankful because it meant my father didn't pay attention to what choices I was making. I didn't want to be a CEO of anything. I just wanted to work with my hands and I had zero interest in marrying and becoming alpha when he died."

"Tanner assured our father over and over that he had no plan to marry Rebecca. She wasn't what my father envisioned for the wife of a successful businessman and alpha. I don't know what Tanner really thought, we weren't that kind of close, but I do know that they seemed to fight and break up as much as they were together. They both slept around when they were on a break and I didn't see that as a sign for future success. I think she knew it too because she started to get more clingy and desperate in the leadup to Tanner's graduation from college. My father started to pay closer attention too and I heard them fighting about her often. Tanner had everything ahead of himself set for success if he just followed our father's plan. So right before graduation he broke up with Rebecca for good, at least it seemed more serious to me. This wasn't a fight where they both yelled at each other, this was him sitting with her and telling her that they were done, that they were on different paths. An alpha needs a strong partner to balance and be in charge with them and she wasn't it in my brother's eyes, or more importantly my father's. I don't know if she would have been or not, honestly."

"She was quiet for about a week but then started calling him again and coming to the house. She was claiming to be pregnant. He told us it was impossible, but I don't think my father believed it and pressured him to take her for an abortion. Tanner tried but she refused, said she was going to have the baby with or without him. She would just keep living with her drunk father next to the house and be part of the pack. Tanner would never be able to get away from her." Onyx paused and looked at Aurora's stomach. "He would have known if it was his," he said thoughtfully. "If he knew it wasn't his then he wouldn't have cared what she did. He must have known, that's why he was so desperate for her to get rid of it. She was threatening the future he'd imagined, the future our father painted for him." Onyx never would have understood if he wasn't sitting next to the woman who was pregnant with his child right now.

Aurora reached out and laid a hand on his. "I'm sure your brother was struggling under all of that pressure."

Onyx nodded in agreement. "There was pressure from her sisters too and even her best friend. Shayla showed up at our door one night screaming about what a horrible family we were to abandon one of our own. She'd just taken Rebecca to the hospital because she'd taken a bunch of pills trying to kill herself, or maybe trying to abort the baby, I'm not sure. I'm not going to lie, in my young mind I imagined it was all for attention, now I don't know, she must have been desperate. My father confronted Tanner about his failure to take care of things quietly. If Rebecca had killed herself while pregnant it would have been a huge scandal and my father hated nothing more than a scandal. Tanner went out and drank too much that night then drove himself into a tree. He died but Rebecca recovered from her ordeal and so did the baby. My father must have felt guilt over it all, not that he'd admit it. I think he saw Rebecca as the girl who held a piece of the son he lost. He didn't question the paternity again but turned his sights on me for all the things he had pictured Tanner for. He decided that I should marry Rebecca."

Aurora gasped in disbelief and knowing she wasn't going to judge him helped him to continue.

"My father felt that I needed to do the duty as the then oldest son to keep the future member of our pack close and safe." Onyx shook his head, remembering how angry his father had been when he refused, how disappointed in him. But all Onyx had seen was his future being ripped away by a woman he didn't love or desire and a heartless father who didn't care what he wanted.

"But you didn't?" she urged him to continue.

"I was given a choice. Marry Rebecca and take my place as head of the house letting my father groom me to take over like he'd been doing with Tanner, or be cut off. I chose to leave. I took every bit of money I'd saved and bought the house next to your grandmother. I was so broke I had to sell sperm for gas money to get there." He shrugged as if it were no big deal. "Now here we are."

"Oh my god, Onyx." Aurora's voice was full of sympathy that warmed him. In all these years he'd never laid out the full story to anyone and had never had anyone tell him that what he'd done was right.

"Yeah, so you can understand why Shayla has some hard feelings toward me and my whole family. It would be too awkward to have her deliver the baby or even be a part of this."

"It does make sense. And all this time, no one has known where you are? Oh my god, Onyx, now they'll know, won't they?"

He didn't tell her that it wasn't completely true, his father had apparently known where he was because when he'd died a lawyer had showed up on Onyx's doorstep. Onyx didn't want to see any more sympathy in her face, that wasn't how he wanted her to look at him. "Isn't there doctor/patient confidentiality?"

"There certainly should be. Maybe we can sue her if she tells anyone she saw us."

He shrugged because suddenly that didn't matter so much. Aurora and the baby mattered, and if more of his past came knocking then they would find out he'd let go of their shitty judgment ages ago.

They stopped for lunch in town because Aurora was starving, her appetite definitely knew she was pregnant today. The only sit-down place Greensferry had was a little diner that had been there for thirty or more years. Luckily it was good and served a few vegetarian options besides salad. They got some funny looks when they entered but this being the third appearance they'd made in town together meant that there was less shock in the faces and more nosy curiosity.

"So you're not a lone wolf by choice, you were forced into this?" Aurora asked after their burgers had been delivered. Hers was a mushroom cap and Swiss cheese, his was beef, rare and double, and he'd added bacon.

"I don't mind being alone, especially considering the alternative."

That didn't settle well with Aurora. He was happy now, but at one point he'd wanted to meet someone, get married, and probably have a whole pack of kids.

If he followed that dream someday then where would that leave her and this little bean?

Why was she even considering welcoming him into this family she was creating if he was going to be looking for something better the whole time? In fact she knew he'd been to the bar since she'd gotten pregnant. The night he came home and demanded his cat. What would it feel like to know he was off at the bar meeting people while she was at home with an infant? She knew she had no right to care, because they weren't in a relationship. So why did it make her throat hurt to think about?

"What is happening in your head?" he asked quietly and reached across the table. The feel of his hot hand on top of hers was a shock and she pulled away immediately.

"Why do you want to be involved with me?" she asked before she could think better of it. "We aren't in a relationship, never were. I am not going to give you a packhouse full of kids and be your little mated wife at home. We probably couldn't even conceive naturally if we tried," she added, a little bit of hysterics creeping into her voice.

Onyx kept his voice low and steady when he spoke. His eyes were locked with hers and she felt it like an anchor she was desperate for but so afraid to take.

"Is that what you think I want? Is that what you got out of my story, Aurora? I have never tried to find a mate. Though yes, as a kid growing up I thought that's what would happen. Kids don't know different than what they see in front of them. But I'm happy alone. And yes, I'm surprised to be in this situation with you, but I am not looking to turn it into more than it is and I have no qualms about you having my child." He hissed the last in a whisper.

Aurora wasn't comforted. He may not be looking to leave her for someone who would be his mate and birth a million children for him, but he didn't really want her either. She focused back on her mushroom burger, already half eaten. "You don't have to do this, no one even has to know it's your baby." She kept her voice low, hoping they weren't outing their situation to the entire town right now, but also knowing that they probably were.

"I'll know," he growled, and the entire place went quiet.

She leaned close and whispered. "But you don't have to claim it, that's what I'm saying. We don't have to acknowledge the truth, Onyx, why do you want to claim this baby?"

"I don't know, Aurora, but I do."

"Instincts," she scoffed and sat back. "You want to force our lives together because of instincts, right?"

"Partly, yes, but also because I'm not a shitty man who would just go around knowing a kid is mine and not doing anything about it."

"So you care what other people think of you, and your animal instincts want you to piss and claim. Do you know how ridiculous that sounds to me as a human woman?"

"I can imagine," he gritted out.

Aurora took a bite of her burger and tried to think reasonably about this. She couldn't possibly understand what he was going through with his instincts but she did know that werewolves made most of their decisions based on them. So did that mean they were less valid decisions than the ones humans made based on feelings?

"Fine," she said.

"Fine?" he asked warily.

"Fine, we can keep doing this together thing. I don't pretend to get it. You don't want a child and you didn't even sleep with me to get this one made, so it's not like you're taking on the consequences of your actions. But I guess if you want to be ruled by your animal instincts, who am I to judge?"

"Fine," he agreed.

They finished their meal in silence.

CHAPTER NINETEEN

Onyx couldn't sleep. The whole day had been so fucked up. He wanted to apologize to Aurora, but he wasn't even sure what he should apologize for. For wanting to be a father to the baby that was his? That didn't seem like the sort of thing to need an apology. He also wanted to snap and snarl at her for even suggesting that he not be a part of the child's life. But he knew that he should be thankful that she was agreeing to let him in the first place.

Selling sperm was neither an intentional creation of a child with a partner, nor was it an accidental one. It was something completely different and he'd signed away his rights to whatever child his sperm created when he'd been in that clinic. Aurora would be well within her rights to tell him to fuck off.

The thought was chilling.

A part of him wanted to truly claim her so that all that other shit would just disappear. That was the part that had him staring at the ceiling unable to rest. He had no idea how to make her his.

A noise from outside drew his attention and he jumped out of bed, thankful for distraction. He hurried to the window and saw that her kitchen light was on. She obviously couldn't sleep either.

Before he could think better of it, he threw on a pair of jeans and a flannel he didn't bother to button up, then went to her back door. He knocked softly and she answered wrapped in a silky robe, hair in a bun, and a cup of tea in her hands. She looked sleepy sexy and his body reacted but he tried to ignore it.

"Is everything alright?" he asked, his voice a little husky.

"Yeah, just having a hard time sleeping," she admitted, her gaze wandering over his exposed chest.

"Anything I can do?" His mind swirled with the possibilities he wanted to present, all of them with her naked.

"No, I was just going to watch a movie until I was tired enough."

"I'll stay," he said, inviting himself in. He wasn't going to give her a chance to deny him, he just entered her space and shut the door behind himself. He hadn't been inside since the morning after the full moon and he wondered if she ever thought about seeing him naked and fully aroused.

"Okay, great. But you have to watch what I picked."

"Of course," he agreed quickly and ushered her into the living room. She had obviously been cuddled up on the couch when he'd knocked. There was a blanket and pillows arranged, and a bowl of popcorn sat on the table that he'd made. Pride filled him knowing she was using something he'd crafted for her. This must be a usual occurrence for her because this was almost exactly what it had looked like when he'd come in on the full moon. Did she have trouble sleeping every night? He didn't like that; it couldn't be good for her or the baby to miss sleep. It did explain why she was often still drinking coffee when he was thinking about lunch though.

Aurora moved to where her blanket lay and he took the spot on the other end of the small couch. She arranged herself against the pillows, fluffing them behind her back, then pulled the blanket over her lower half. She hit play on the television and a movie he wasn't sure if he recognized started to play, not that it mattered, he could only concentrate on her.

He was aware of every movement she made and every time she laughed; he really liked her laugh. It was easy to tell when she was starting to fall asleep because her leg twitched and suddenly her feet were pressed against him. He stiffened, unwilling to move and disturb the contact. He glanced at her through his periphery and saw her eyes drooping but she was fighting it.

He gently pulled her feet onto his lap, allowing her head to slip down further on the couch.

"What?" she asked, her eyes widening at him.

"Get cozy, you need to fall asleep, right? I'm not here to disturb you, just keep you company."

She nodded and settled into the new position. His hands were still on her feet and he started to rub them, delighting in the soft feel of her skin. He concentrated on making his movements slow and firm, lulling her toward the sleep she needed. When her breathing was deep and even he continued, not wanting to give up the contact. He studied her without shame as she slept. His eyes trailed over her soft face and down her body, mostly covered though it was by a blanket.

She was a very pretty woman, and she was fierce and smart. She was also independent and brave. She was everything he would have picked for himself if he'd ever felt like picking someone to be his mate and mother of his children. If she'd also been a werewolf.

His eyes dipped to where her stomach lay under the blanket, flat as ever of course. But soon it would be swelling with his child. He wondered what the child would be like. Would it shift, would it crave raw meat under the full moon? Would it be full of light and cheer like its mother?

Would he love it either way?

That was an easy answer, he knew he would, he already did. He could feel the draw to it, and her. The scent of his child growing in her womb was intoxicating and pulled on all of his instincts. That wouldn't change much after it was born. He'd be driven to protect the child. He wondered if this draw to *her* would end. Would he only be left with the desire to protect someone important to his child's survival, a member of his pack? Would all the desire he felt now to claim her end with the birth of the child? He didn't know for sure and that worried him.

Aurora woke up the next morning in her bed, but she was certain she hadn't put herself there. She vaguely remembered Onyx massaging her feet on the couch, and then nothing. She must have been exhausted to have slept through him moving her. She wondered if it would ever stop surprising her that he could be sweet and caring. She supposed it was good to know, since she'd want those qualities in a father for her child. She tried not to think about how much she wanted those qualities in a partner for herself too.

She spent the morning researching other OB-GYNs in the area and contacted two possibilities to see if they had openings for new clients. By lunch she was starving and ate way too much, then collapsed on the couch for a lazy afternoon while her stomach tried to rebel. She supposed it wasn't too early to start feeling the effects of pregnancy. Her boobs hurt, her period was long missed, and her appetite had been off for a couple days. Morning sickness was no surprise and she welcomed the additional sign that life was growing inside of her.

She must have fallen asleep because the next thing she knew, the sun was setting and she was hungry again. She sat up on the couch and her head whirled so she laid back down. She needed some water and some crackers, and an ice cream sandwich. But getting up seemed like a dangerous feat at the moment.

Her phone was within reach and before she could talk herself out of it, she grabbed it and sent a text to Onyx.

Hey, if you're not busy could you come over here?

She expected a text back, but he walked through the front door less than a minute later. He was sweaty and bare chested, covered in sawdust and looking like a wet dream.

"What's wrong?" he demanded.

She forced her eyes up to his face and gave a half smile. "Oh, uh, nothing really. It's just that I'm feeling a little light-headed and I was hoping you could grab me some water and crackers. I think if I get up myself right now I might puke or pass out."

He growled as he went into the kitchen and she regretted texting him. She was doing this on her own, she shouldn't have bothered him. It wasn't his job to take care of her and if she abused his—well she wouldn't call it niceness—feelings of obligation maybe? If she abused it he might not be willing to help if she really needed it. She sat up slowly this time and her head only slightly spun, telling her that she could have just waited a minute and been fine to take care of herself. She didn't need him to wait on her and he didn't need to be bothered from his work.

"Sorry," she said when he handed her the water and crackers. He'd also grabbed some cheese. "I shouldn't have texted you. I was just being silly."

He grunted. "You probably need some protein if your stomach can handle it."

She hated that he was right. Her mouth watered looking at the cheese and she forgot all about the ice cream sandwich she'd been craving. Almost ... she would have that when he left and couldn't judge her.

"Don't be sorry, I told you to text me if you needed anything."

"Yeah but still, I'm not helpless."

He gave her a look that clearly said he disagreed with that statement.

"I'm not," she argued.

"I will make you dinner."

She opened her mouth to tell him that wasn't necessary but he growled at her and she slammed her mouth shut.

"Eat," he demanded and she did.

After she'd finished most of what he'd brought her he looked satisfied and stood.

"I am going to go clean up my project and shower. I'll be back to make dinner."

Part of her screamed to deny him this, but another part of her was so happy to have someone want to do nice things for her that she just nodded. "Thank you, Onyx, I'm sorry I texted you. I would have been fine if I'd just waited a couple minutes and sat up slower. I know now for next time."

"It's stupid to risk hurting yourself or the baby just because you didn't want to text me," he said and walked out of the house.

She seethed as the door closed. Did he just call her stupid? She grabbed her phone and called Claire.

"No, he said you would be stupid to not take his offered help, and I agree, Aurora. If he wants to play sexy waiter while you're creating life inside your womb with his sperm, let him. There has to be some kind of advantage to this whole situation, right?"

"I guess so, I just feel like I shouldn't need him," she admitted with a sigh.

"Honestly, you don't. You are a strong independent woman who took control of her own fertility and motherhood. You don't need him, but that doesn't mean you can't use him," she said with an innuendo Aurora didn't miss.

"I am not going to sleep with the man just because he brought me crackers."

"I agree, you should sleep with him because he's fucking hot and you're going to be horny at some point in the next seven months."

And then she'd be a mom and too tired to date. That was the unsaid portion of Claire's comment and it was depressing.

Aurora sighed. "Want to meet for lunch tomorrow?"

"Sure, if your baby daddy will let you out of his sight," she teased.

Aurora wanted to roll her eyes but she knew it would be an issue. "Well if not, he can tag along. What's more fun on a girl's lunch date than a glaring man?"

Claire laughed and Aurora was reminded of why she'd called her friend. Claire always made her feel better, no matter the situation.

CHAPTER TWENTY

Onyx dressed in his cleanest jeans and T-shirt and pulled his hair up rather than leaving it loose since he would be cooking. Then he crossed to Aurora's house with all the ingredients in hand to make a vegetable stir fry and rice. It was quick and easy and something he'd practiced making. He would have liked to make her a spinach salad too, but he needed to go into town for more fresh vegetables. He usually satisfied himself with frozen so he could avoid shopping more than once a month but he wanted to provide fresh food for her. If he could have gone out and hunted some meat and brought it to her he would have. Instead he'd hunt in town for vegetables that would please and nourish her, although it was not as satisfying to his wolf who didn't understand her dietary preferences.

It meant he was going into town way more often than usual. Aurora and her baby were changing almost everything he'd set his life up to be out here. He wasn't sure why that didn't piss him off more.

She answered the door with a smile lighting up her face, which was gaining a bit of color from the sun he noticed, it really highlighted her freckles. She was wearing a simple black cotton dress, but it was stunning on her. Her hair hung loose around her face and he ached to wrap his hands in it.

She stepped aside to let him in and as always when he entered her home he was assaulted by the scent of her, pregnant her, and his growing child. It made him never want to leave.

"Is everything okay?" she asked and he realized he'd frozen one step inside the house.

"I'm making vegetables and rice," he answered and forced himself to walk into the kitchen. He opened the window there first, hoping a little fresh evening air would help calm his pounding heart. All it did was remind him that her house wasn't marked well enough, that his scent wasn't pervasive on the wind around her property.

She was unprotected and vulnerable to predators and suitors.

"Thanks again for earlier," she said from the doorway. "I really appreciate it, and I won't abuse your willingness to help, I swear."

"Asking for help isn't a weakness," he said.

"Right, well, still. I will get used to all the little things, I'm sure. Next time I nap I'll maybe have water and crackers nearby for when I wake up."

He grunted, wanting to tell her not to. He wanted to tell her to just call him, text him, let him sleep at her feet and be there when she woke up.

His chest rumbled at the thought and his cock twitched. He forced his mind to the task at hand. He was here to feed her, not bed her.

"Are you sure you're okay?" she asked, a little closer now.

"I am."

"Okay well, is there anything I can do to help?"

He nearly groaned at the offer. If she were his mate he'd tell her she could suck his cock and then let him eat her out and fuck her hard before he hand fed her.

But she wasn't. So he only shook his head and tried to angle his hips away from her view so she couldn't see the raging hard on he was now sporting like a teenager.

"Alright," she said and wandered out of the kitchen.

He managed to cook the meal and settle his body. As they ate she told him she planned to head to town the next day to meet Claire for lunch.

"I'll go with you."

"You don't have to, it'll be all girl talk."

"I need to go to the store anyway. One trip will be better," he insisted. There was no way he was letting her go without him.

"Sure," she agreed, not seeming excited about it, but resigned to his company. That was not what he wanted, a woman resigned to his company. It felt shitty and it made him angry. Angry at her and really fucking angry at those witches and that meddling goddess who did this to them.

"We should sue the company," he said suddenly.

"What?"

"The fertility clinic. We should talk to a lawyer. They shouldn't have been able to do this to us."

"We can't, there is a clause in the contract I signed, probably yours too. A chaos clause that basically says if the goddess intervenes, we can't sue."

Onyx growled.

"Is it really that terrible? Me having your baby?" she asked, her voice tight with emotions that made his own heart ache.

"No, it's not that terrible," he admitted. It was complicated, and it was changing how he felt about her and his life. It made him want things that he thought he'd given up on years ago.

"You don't have to be a part of it," she said, something she'd mentioned before as if she had no idea that that was an impossibility for a werewolf.

He gave her a look that statement deserved. "If I could walk away, don't you think I would?" he snarled.

"Fuck you, Onyx," she snapped back and stood. "I think I've had enough of your delightful company for one night, get out."

He wanted to tell her no, but he knew she had every right to tell him to leave. This was her house and he was a guest. He took his plate to the sink and left knowing he had made a mistake. He had held back because he was afraid she'd laugh in his face if he told her he wanted her and not just the child. Something he was barely admitting to himself.

Aurora was seething as she did the dishes. Somehow knowing he'd made a really great vegetarian meal made her even more angry. Why did he have to swing so wide? Why was he so hot and cold with her?

One minute it was like he was trying to sort of date her and the next he was acting like she'd ruined his life on purpose.

She called her mom and poured out her heart.

"It sounds to me like he doesn't know what he wants. Werewolves run pretty hot with their emotions so it's not surprising that he's reacting big. What *is* surprising is that he has those moments of calm and soft with you. That tells me something."

"Is it that he's a fucking psychopath?"

Her mother laughed. "No, it tells me those are his true feelings but he's trying very hard to keep them at bay."

"Is this like the old *If a boy pulls your pigtails it's because he likes you,* bullshit? Because I thought as a society we've come to realize that that is what makes women accept abusive relationships far too easily."

"No, this is all about him. He's been a loner for a long time and this is an unexpected disruption to his quiet life. He's having feelings for you, unexpected feelings, and he doesn't know how to deal with it. I don't think that gives him a right to be an ass and you should tell him as much. Let him know what you will and will not accept from him. And if he doesn't keep to those boundaries, then kick his ass to the curb."

Aurora sighed. "But what if I don't know what I want from him?"

"Then you need to figure that out fast because you're about to have bigger things to deal with than your love life, sweetie."

"Which is why I didn't want a love life involved in this baby thing."

"The universe chooses for us sometimes, doesn't it?"

"Yes, it does," Aurora agreed.

She went to bed with her mother's advice running through her mind. She knew the woman was right. She needed to decide what she wanted from Onyx, then she needed to lay out the things she'd accept from him and let him decide what he would do.

But what did she want? Her horny body wanted his, but her brain was sure he was going to always be a bit of an ass and that wasn't acceptable. Her heart was oddly quiet though and she had a feeling that was because it didn't want to fess up to what it hoped for.

CHAPTER TWENTY-ONE

Aurora was up early and out of the house dressed in one of her favorite bright yellow sun dresses with her hair in two braids. Onyx didn't usually sleep in but she hadn't spotted him yet. She hoped he wasn't ill, but she also wanted to get away before he could jump in her car. She hadn't come to any real decisions last night and until she did, she didn't even want to look at him.

It was mid-week market day in Greensferry and she always enjoyed walking through the local vendor booths and picking up seasonal treats. It was a good activity to clear her mind. Maybe if she got away from him and his scent that wafted over from his house, a scent that her pregnancy nose was able to pick up far too easily, she'd be able to sort through some of what she was feeling.

She parked next to a coffee stand and Claire was already there waiting with a cup of tea for her.

"Are we expecting an angry neighbor?" Claire asked as Aurora took the tea. Claire had dressed in cutoff shorts and a tank-top that advertised a local bar that her brother owned.

"At some point, I don't doubt it," she admitted but took the tea gratefully and held up her market basket. "But if he wants to be a fool, he can. I am shopping and looking forward to lunch and talking."

"Dinner didn't go well?"

"Dinner went well, but after that he was his usual asshole self and I am just so tired of it. He needs to pick a lane."

"And which lane is it you'd like him to pick?" Claire prompted.

"I don't know," Aurora whined because that was the biggest problem. If she knew what she wanted from him she would tell him.

Claire gave her a sympathetic side hug and they started down the row of vendors.

They strolled through the market and Aurora happily filled her basket with early season veggies. The sun felt amazing on her skin and she didn't even think about Onyx, at least she tried not to. It was nearly impossible when every shadow in the corner of her eye had her turning to see if it was him and Claire watched her with a half-smile as if she knew exactly what was going on in Aurora's head.

"Well look what I found. The two cutest girls in town," Steven said with a slimy grin as he sidled up to them at a jam booth.

"Steven," Claire said with a sharp dismissal.

"Wow, Aurora. You look like you bought enough for three, are you planning to have me over for dinner?" His eyes landed on her chest as he spoke.

She wished she'd worn a dress with a looser fit on top and she resented him for making her feel like her fashion choices weren't about being comfortable with herself. Her breasts had grown a little already and it was a hot day. She felt cute and comfortable when she left the house, but he made her regret not dressing for safety. She wanted to tell him that she wouldn't invite him over if he was the last man on earth, but she settled for something he would definitely understand. "I am repaying Onyx for a few meals he cooked me. He's taking great care of me since he found out I'm pregnant."

"Pregnant …" Steven said, eyeing her flat stomach with a wariness that belonged on the face of a man who could possibly be the father, not a man who she'd never let so much as buy her a cup of coffee.

"Yep, I'm all knocked up," she said with glee as his eyes finally made it up to her face.

"And Onyx is taking care of you, why?" he asked, suddenly suspicious.

"Because it's my baby," Onyx growled, appearing beside her seemingly out of nowhere.

Steven huffed and puffed out his chest. "I thought you were smarter than to let this asshole in your pants. Apparently I shouldn't have been so nice and maybe I would have gotten a run at that womb myself," Steven sneered.

The words were followed immediately by a feral growl and Onyx leaping through the air.

"Onyx, no," Aurora screamed as Steven was taken to the ground under Onyx's body.

Claire rushed forward, arm extended, and then there was a buzz and Onyx started to shake. Steven crawled out from under Onyx's now limp body, nose bleeding and eyes watering. Aurora didn't have an ounce of sympathy for the creep.

Steven scowled at Aurora and spit a mass of blood and mucus on Onyx's back. "Fucking psycho," he gritted then glared at her. "Good luck having a baby with that," he said and walked away at a fast pace.

A crowd had gathered which meant the whole town was about to know what was going on with her and Onyx. It also meant security would be on the way, but Aurora didn't care about either. She sank to her knees next to Onyx who had rolled to his back with a groan. "Are you okay?" she asked, her hands shaking with the desire to touch him but afraid he'd react badly.

"What the hell was that?" he groaned.

"Stun gun, got it from an ex-cop," Claire said brightly. "It's got enough voltage to take down a werewolf."

"I see that," he groaned again and sat up. Aurora reached out to help him and he didn't brush her away.

"What the hell were you thinking?" she demanded when it was obvious he wasn't really harmed.

He growled at the crowd which promptly dispersed. "I was thinking that Steven is an asshole who deserves to have his ass beat."

"Agreed," Claire said.

"No, violence is not the way to handle him, he's just an idiot."

The security arrived then. It was just a couple of young men who looked like they were barely out of high school and unreliable with a weapon. Claire gave them cheerful smiles and started to explain what had happened in a way that definitely put all the blame on Steven and left out the part where Claire had stunned Onyx.

They seemed satisfied with that, especially since Steven wasn't there to complain or press charges. No doubt investigating further would just mean paperwork for them.

Aurora gave them appreciative smiles and led Onyx to a bench where she handed him what was left of her tea.

"Drink this," she ordered.

"You're mad," he pointed out but took the tea and sipped it.

"I know how to handle assholes. I'm a grown woman so obviously I've been doing it for years," she chastised.

"Just because you *can* do something on your own, doesn't mean you should have to," Onyx said.

Aurora felt like he was talking about a hell of a lot more than just Steven's negative reaction to rejection. She also felt like she wasn't ready to go there so she just huffed. "Do you have some shopping to do?"

"Yes."

"Great," she grumbled and started to walk, grabbing Claire's arm. If Onyx wanted to follow them like a guard dog then she wouldn't bother stopping him.

Onyx stuck close to Aurora as she and Claire meandered through the rest of the market, and even joined them for lunch. It wasn't entirely unpleasant, but his skin itched with the feeling of being watched and judged. He knew what the townspeople thought of him, and he didn't really care because he wasn't interested in being their friend. But the way that so many of them glanced at Aurora with worry had him internally cringing. She was a social person, and she thrived on interactions with these people. But because of him being with her, he knew she wasn't getting what she normally would out of a day like this.

Had he ruined her good time? All he wanted to do was keep her safe.

"Oh, let's go in there. I need to find a new table for my back porch," Claire said, pointing to an antiques shop.

Onyx frowned at the shop. It looked like the type of place that had more junk than actual antiques.

"You won't find anything good in there," he said.

"And you're the expert on what's good?" Claire asked with a snort and went into the shop.

"She knows I make furniture," Onyx grumbled as Aurora followed her friend inside.

"But you don't sell it this cheap," Aurora pointed out as she held the door for him.

"Who wants cheap furniture?" he scoffed.

"Poor teachers," Aurora said with a laugh.

Onyx didn't lose his scowl as he prowled behind the women who took their sweet time going up and down every aisle.

Claire stopped at a baby pram that looked like it was falling apart and cooed. "Oh my god, Aurora, next summer we'll be pushing one of these down the street with us."

"That's a death trap," he snarled.

Claire just rolled her eyes. "Obviously we won't be buying this exact one. She'll probably need a two or three seater anyway, what with having a whole litter."

"Not funny," Aurora said, but she was smiling. "You know werewolves are just as unlikely to have multiples as humans are."

"It doesn't run in my family," Onyx admitted.

"Not in mine either, so I'm guessing we will only need a single stroller."

"And so many other things. We really should start a registry and watch for sales on cribs and car seats and all those big ticket items," Claire said. They walked on, talking of all the baby items Aurora would need as if Claire were the father instead of him. It grated on his nerves and there was a sly look on Claire's face that made him wonder if she were doing it on purpose.

Onyx's mind started to spin around all of it and maybe that was her point. He hadn't considered how much prep would go into getting ready for the baby. All of the things that would have to be purchased and arranged before Aurora even gave birth.

And she was a poor teacher. Why the hell had she been thinking about doing it all on her own?

"We should get married." The words were out of his mouth before he could stop them. He focused and realized he'd followed the two into the large furniture area of the store and the owner was standing with them now, talking about a table Claire might want.

"Sorry, you're not my type," Claire said breaking the silence.

Aurora just stared at him with eyes wide and mouth gaping.

Frank, the store owner, looked just as shocked.

"You don't make enough to support yourself and the child," he reasoned.

"Wow, um, as romantic as *that* was, I'll pass," Aurora said.

Onyx's body heated with embarrassment, but he also knew he wasn't wrong. Aurora would need help. He was the obvious choice to help because he was the father of the child.

"Babies are expensive," he pointed out.

"Do you think I'm an idiot?" Aurora asked carefully.

Onyx panicked, this was a trap. He looked at Claire who was grinning wide and then to Frank who was slowly backing away with a look of terror on his face. When he looked back to Aurora her face was too calm. She had one eyebrow cocked and her arms were crossed. She was waiting for an answer and he thought he knew what some of her students felt like when they tried to give her the *dog ate my essay* excuse.

"You're not an idiot. I'm just saying that I am the father and I want to help."

"If I needed help, Onyx, then I wouldn't have gone to the sperm bank."

"I know but—"

She held up a hand, cutting off his excuses. "I think we're done with your escort today." She turned and walked away.

He was about to follow but Claire stepped in front of him.

"Dude, that was probably the dumbest thing I've ever heard in my life. Aurora doesn't suffer fools very well so you better give her some space." Claire patted his arm, more amusement than sympathy on her face, and then turned to follow Aurora.

Frank stood nearby looking at him sympathetically and Onyx had an urge to bite the man's head off for having witnessed his embarrassment. He settled for baring his teeth in the man's direction which had him scrambling into the back room.

Onyx slunk out of the store feeling like he had his tail between his legs. He really was an idiot. But he refused to leave town while she was there so he headed to Jordan's nursery.

"Wow, who kicked you?" Gertrude asked when he approached her between the rows of potted fruit trees and bushes.

"No one."

"Ah, even worse, you acted a fool, didn't you?"

"Maybe."

"Well why don't you help me unload the rest of these trees from the truck and you can tell me about it."

Onyx nodded and followed the witch. After ten minutes of physical activity he told her about how he'd attacked Steven and then proposed to Aurora. He admitted that it was more than just his desire to make sure she was financially okay, he also wanted to make sure she was marked as his.

"And that is the hardest part about not dating your own species, isn't it? She doesn't understand the werewolf instincts to protect and provide," Gertrude said calmly.

"They are stronger than I would have expected," he admitted.

"Perhaps you need to talk to someone who's gone through it. I don't know what brought you out here to Greensferry, Onyx. I know you live alone and without a pack or family, but is there anyone who you might be able to talk to about what you're feeling?"

Onyx knew she was right, but who could he talk to? He'd purposely avoided making any connections here.

CHAPTER TWENTY-TWO

"You know he's just a big dumb animal, right?" Claire said.

"I know," Aurora sighed as she put her purchases in the back of her car. "But that doesn't mean I have to put up with bullshit, or wolf shit."

"Definitely not. Call me if he proposes again," Claire laughed and hugged Aurora.

Aurora laughed too because what else could she do?

When she pulled out of town she was not even a little surprised to see Onyx's truck behind her. "Stalker," she mumbled, then turned up the radio and ignored him and the way his determination to watch over her made her feel warm and fuzzy.

He of course rushed to her as soon as they were parked at home. He reached out to take the bag of veggies in her arms but she held tight, not willing to just forget.

He growled. "I shouldn't have assumed you were unable to provide what is necessary to have a child that you obviously conceived on purpose," he said.

She had to swallow her retort because this was his way of apologizing. "No, you shouldn't have," she agreed and let him take the bag. She grabbed the jars of honey and jam she'd purchased and followed him into her kitchen.

"Did Claire find a table?" he asked as he put away the vegetables. "You should have gotten spinach, you need the iron," he added as he started to pull items out of her bags.

Aurora bared her teeth at his back but chose to ignore the second remark. "No, she wasn't able to find something sturdy and in her price range."

He grunted and turned to look at her. "What are you having for dinner?"

"Not spinach," she snapped.

He had the audacity to look surprised by her reaction.

"Onyx, you don't get to control me or this pregnancy."

"I know," he gritted.

"Do you?" she challenged.

He nodded once.

"I'm going to take a nap," she said and walked away.

She heard him leave as she laid down on her bed. She really was tired, pregnancy was no joke even this early. Which reminded her that she needed to find a new doctor and she needed to think about what kind of birth she wanted and classes to go along with it. She needed to let the school know so they could plan for a long-term sub and she needed to decide if she was going to turn the office into a nursery or just use half her bedroom since she lived alone anyway.

She drifted to sleep with so many thoughts running through her mind she woke up right where she'd left off two hours later. Did she want to circumcise it if it was a boy?

Her eyes snapped open and she frowned at the ceiling. Did werewolves circumcise? She knew Onyx wasn't, she'd seen it for herself when he'd dropped his towel in his living room.

The memory had her body heating so she had to think about all the things about him that were annoying. He gave short answers and he glowered. He pissed in her yard and he made a lot of noise early in the morning. And he didn't like anything about her, he complained about her and glared at her.

But she had poisoned him and he hadn't lashed out at her, he just doubled his efforts to protect her. Why?

And how did you get an overprotective werewolf to give you some space?

"Step one is probably don't be pregnant with his baby," she grumbled as she rolled out of her bed and headed for the kitchen.

She froze when she saw a huge bowl of fresh spinach sitting on her counter. Tears burned her eyes. She wasn't sure if it was because she was so pissed off by his heavy handed treatment of her diet or if it was because he cared enough that he went back to town, a place he hated to be, and got spinach for her while she napped.

"Damn pregnancy hormones." She wiped her eyes and pulled out some eggs to make a quiche.

Onyx picked up his phone and made a phone call he didn't think he'd ever make. He didn't have his childhood best friend's current phone number, but it didn't take long for him to figure out the man owned a coffee shop and bakery with his wife in Oceanview. He dialed the store and waited, his palms sweating and his throat tightening.

"Mooncalled Coffee," a female voice answered.

"Is Glen there?"

"Just a minute. Glen," the voice yelled in the distance.

Onyx almost panicked and hung up but then a voice said *hello* that brought back a hundred wonderful memories.

"Hello?" Glen said again.

"Glen, it's me, um—"

"Fucking goddess is that you, Onyx?"

A lump formed in his throat and he had to clear it before he could answer. "Yeah, it's me."

"Are you okay? What do you need, where are you?" Glen's rapid-fire questions had Onyx tightening his grip on the phone. He wasn't prepared to answer questions, only ask them.

"I'm good, I've been lone wolfing it."

"I know. I understand why you left too, but why didn't you ever come back?"

"I had to get away from my father's expectations of me."

"I get that, man." Glen cleared his throat then. "You know he died a few years back?"

"I know."

"I've missed you. I wanted to share so many things with you over the years."

"I saw the pictures on your business website. You are a real family wolf."

"I am," Glen said proudly. "What about you?"

Onyx took a deep breath. "That's actually why I called. I need some advice. Have you talked to your sister?"

"Shayla? Not in a few weeks, why?"

Onyx was relieved and surprised that Shayla hadn't gone straight to tattle on him to her older brother. Onyx explained the insane situation he was in.

"No shit? You're not going to believe this, but Martha's best friend is the woman who got knocked up with the vampire sperm there just last year. It was the same situation, a switch of sperm on her at the last minute."

"Did she sue?"

"No, there's a clause, as I'm sure you know. And it worked out anyway. The goddess knows what she's doing, even if she chooses to do it in the most chaotic fashion possible."

"That's true," Onyx agreed, this did feel chaotic, he was reserving judgment on whether it was a good thing or not.

"If you're worried at all, my wife and mother-in-law would be happy to do a little communion with the Moon Goddess if you bring Aurora over."

"I'm not sure I could convince her to do that, she's a little pissed at me right now. That's why I called. I don't know what is going on with me."

Glen laughed. "When Martha got pregnant with our first I thought I was going insane. I couldn't let her out of my sight without panicking and I pissed on every inch of our property. She got so mad she left one day and spent a week hiding from me. Of course, I knew where she was and I sat outside the hotel snarling the whole time. But she pretended I wasn't there and when she came home she told me if I didn't calm the fuck down she was going to fly somewhere and good luck finding her then. It was enough to get my attention. I forced my wolf to calm his shit and we survived. The next kid was easier."

"So your advice is that I just ignore my instincts?"

"Yeah, as best you can. Just let her lead. What is she wanting and willing to put up with as far as your need to protect goes? I mean, it helped that I kept Martha well marked and slept with her in my arms."

"That's not happening," he growled, but he knew it would help. His wolf was perking up at the idea already and his cock was hardening. If he could mark her, then he'd feel better about things. "I did have the stupid idea today to propose."

"I'm guessing she didn't take well to that idea."

"Not at all. She is just so damn independent, she doesn't need me at all."

"Which has you trying everything possible I'm guessing?"

He admitted that he was.

"I suggest you talk to her about expectations and boundaries. This isn't what either of you planned but now you're in it. It's not much different than a one-night stand turning into a pregnancy. You have to figure out what it means for you both."

"I don't remember you being this insightful in high school when you were encouraging me to pound five beers and take the skateboard off the pier."

Glen laughed. "Being a father changes you."

They said their goodbyes then and exchanged numbers. Onyx promised to visit the next time he was in town and Glen promised not to tell anyone about Aurora.

Onyx was working on a project when Aurora approached with a plate of food. "I made too much," she said in explanation as she held it out with a smile. He wasn't sure it wasn't poisoned but he took it anyway.

"Spinach quiche," he said with a grunt as he wiped his hands on his dirty pants and took the plate. He wanted to say something about how she should eat it because she needed the protein and iron but thought better of it.

He took a big bite and as soon as he did, she asked, "Do werewolves circumcise?"

He coughed and choked on the food, knowing she'd intentionally waited until he had a mouthful to ask *that* question. She just watched him with that damn smile on her face.

He narrowed his eyes at her as he fought his way through it and swallowed. "No."

She nodded. "That's what I thought." Her eyes dipped down to his crotch and back up so fast he knew she hoped he wouldn't notice, but he did, and he gave her a half smile. If she wanted to see it again, he'd be more than happy to show her.

"You can bring the plate back when you're done," she said with pink cheeks and walked back to her house.

He finished the quiche in two bites and then got his project cleaned up. Just as he was about to take the plate back to her she hurried back out onto the porch and his heart froze.

Something was wrong.

CHAPTER TWENTY-THREE

Aurora clung to her purse and looked across at Onyx, thankful he was still outside, there was no time to waste. "I need you to take me to the hospital," she said, her voice hitching and tears on her cheeks.

He didn't say anything, just ran to her and picked her up, then ran to his truck. She was buckling in as he pulled out of the driveway. "Which hospital?" he asked as they sped toward town.

"Actually the birthing center I think. I know it's a little further but I think—I think that makes more sense."

"You?" he said and she realized he must have assumed someone was hurt that she needed to get to.

"I don't know what's wrong," she sobbed.

Onyx reached across the bench seat and unbuckled her then pulled her against him. She curled into his side as best she could and cried, terrified of what was happening in her body.

Onyx didn't speak as he drove and his arm never let go of her. The comfort was everything she needed right then and so were his driving skills. He got them to the clinic in half the time it should have taken. He parked with a jerk and pulled her into his arms, carrying her inside. She clung to him as if he could do a damn thing to really help her, but she knew if he wasn't there she'd fall apart.

"We need help," he demanded.

Nurses rushed forward but he refused to let her down to be wheeled away and she refused to unbury her face from his chest to say anything. Finally, they let him walk her to a room where he gently set her on a bed. She didn't want to leave him though, she held on.

"Hey, I've got you. I'm not going anywhere, Aurora, but they need to look at you. I'm not leaving your side," he promised.

She hated it, she didn't want to separate from him even a little. He was sharing his strength with her and she needed that, but he was right, she needed the doctors too. She let go of him but as promised he stayed right there next to the bed. She grabbed his hand and her eyes darted around the room that was set up for birthing mothers. Fresh tears fell down her face and Onyx squeezed her hand tighter.

"What happened?" a nurse asked Onyx and Aurora saw panic on his face as he admitted he had no idea.

They both turned to look at her.

"There was blood," she sobbed. "I went to the bathroom and there was blood, so much blood. Am I losing the baby? Did I already lose the baby?" She was so terrified. She wanted this baby, werewolf and all, she wanted it. If she lost it she didn't think she'd ever recover. This was her little bean, her baby, her little wolf pup.

The door opened and Onyx growled as Dr. Blithe came in the room. Of course it had to be her.

"What's going on, Aurora?" Shayla asked with a calm tone and grabbed her hand, checking her pulse while the nurse used one of those forehead thermometers on her.

Onyx explained this time. "Is Aurora going to be okay?" he asked.

Shayla ignored him. "What about pain, Aurora? Scale of one to ten."

"No pain," Aurora said.

Shayla made a hum noise and then set down her wrist. "Okay, that's good."

"How can that be good?" Onyx demanded with a snarl.

Shayla continued to ignore him and kept her eyes on Aurora. "Sometimes there's bleeding. That doesn't mean anything is wrong, but we do need to check. Now, I need you to be very honest with me, Aurora." For the first time Shayla looked briefly at Onyx. "Did you encounter any kind of trauma, any bumps or hits, any *falls*?"

She was asking if Onyx had hurt her, Aurora realized, and it pissed her off. How dare this woman accuse Onyx of such a thing? The man was annoying and grumpy, but he wasn't violent. "No," she snapped.

Shayla nodded as if she'd expected that answer. "I have to ask and if there's anything more you want to talk about, alone, you let someone know," she said as Onyx growled.

"No, just please tell me the baby is okay," Aurora pleaded.

"We will do a scan, how far along are you?"

"About eight weeks."

"Great, that means we should get a good look with a regular ultrasound, nothing invasive. Pull up your shirt and push your skirt down a little. The baby is still really low," Shayla explained.

Shayla faced Onyx and something passed between them that Aurora didn't have the energy to decipher, then Shayla was walking out. A nurse hooked Aurora up to a monitor and Onyx pulled a chair over to sit by her side without ever letting go of her hand.

"I'm scared," she said, staring up at the ceiling.

"Me too," he said.

She looked at him, surprised at the admission. She searched his face for any sign that he was lying or that he was hoping that this would end the pregnancy and he would get out of being her baby's father. But all she saw was fear.

Aurora went back to staring at the ceiling, praying to the Moon Goddess for her baby's health.

Shayla returned quickly with the ultrasound machine. The nurse got it plugged in and turned on while Shayla squirted warm goo on Aurora's stomach.

Aurora had imagined this moment a million times since she decided that she was going to have a baby. She imagined the excitement and anticipation, she'd imagined having her mother with her or Claire. In none of those imaginings had she thought she'd feel this deep aching worry, or this solid comforting presence. She squeezed Onyx's hand tighter.

"Do you want to watch the screen?" Shayla asked quietly.

The unsaid was, or do you not want to see that there's nothing but an empty womb where a baby used to be.

"I want to see," Aurora said firmly. Onyx squeezed her hand.

Shayla turned the screen in their direction then began the ultrasound. It was nothing but a dark blur and fresh tears flowed down Aurora's face. Onyx squeezed her hand tighter and with his other, wiped them away.

Then a sound filled the room, a strong bum-bum-bum.

"There's a heartbeat," Shayla said, and Aurora let out a loud sob.

Onyx leaned down and kissed her cheek. "It's a strong beat, werewolves have strong hearts," he whispered in her ear.

"This is the baby," Shayla said pointing to the screen then pushed a few buttons. "It's measuring right on track for eight and a half weeks. This is the placenta here, it looks healthy. Did you ever have an IUD?"

"Yes, for quite a few years when I was in my twenties."

Shayla sat back and the screen went blank. "I can't say for sure what the bleeding was, but sometimes the placenta tries to grow over a scar in the uterus. An IUD can cause some scarring within the uterus. Did you have any issues with it at insertion or removal?"

"Yes actually, it was stuck in the wall, which I found out when it was removed."

"You're lucky you were able to get pregnant after that. Sometimes it can cause infertility, but it isn't dangerous now. Likely that was the bleeding, but I want you to be very careful over the next week and if you see any more bleeding, come in again right away and we'll do more tests." She turned to Onyx then. "You'll be around in case she needs help?"

"I will," he agreed.

She nodded approvingly at him. "Aurora, I expect you to have a healthy baby," she said with a genuine smile.

"Thank you, Dr. Blithe."

"Of course, just doing my job," she said with a shrug and stood.

Awkwardness filled the room then, because she *was* doing her job, and it hadn't mattered that she had a history of not liking Onyx's family.

"I'm sorry we walked out of the clinic," Aurora said.

"No problem, I get it," she shrugged.

"But I'd like you to be my doctor. I want a werewolf doctor, I have so many questions," she admitted.

Shayla turned to her with surprise on her face. "I'd like that, but are *you* okay with it?" she asked Onyx.

"You seem to know what you're doing, and Aurora deserves the best care. If you think you can give her that, then I am fine with whatever she wants."

"Typical werewolf male, vaguely threatening to get their mate the best care." She rolled her eyes at Aurora. "The nurses will be in with some paperwork. I'll see you at my office in a couple weeks."

. . .

Onyx gave Aurora a reassuring look before following Shayla out of the room. She turned to face him in the hall, arms crossed and face blank. She didn't speak first.

"Thank you," Onyx said.

Her eyes widened slightly at his words. "I didn't do anything."

"You were calm and kind and reassuring. You were exactly what she needed in there and … me too I guess."

"I read her file, I know this was artificial insemination."

"It doesn't matter. It's my child in there."

"I have no doubt it is. You wouldn't care otherwise, would you?" she snapped then took a breath, regaining her professional composure. "It doesn't answer the question of why you care so much about what happens to Aurora. You aren't just concerned for the child, you care about her."

"Of course, she's the mother of my child."

"It's more than that. Your focus was on how Aurora was, not the baby, she was your first concern."

"I can't lose her," he admitted and he knew it was the absolute truth.

"Well, you haven't yet, but can I give you some advice?"

He wanted to say no but nodded.

"Let her know how you feel."

He didn't have a response for that. "Thank you for not telling Glen."

"Do you really think I'd risk losing my job over you?" she snarled.

"I don't know what I thought."

"Do you know what your problem is, Onyx? You expect the worst out of this life."

"Life has shown me some shit," he admitted then turned and walked back into the room.

Aurora was crying again when he walked in and he growled at the nurse who was putting away the ultrasound equipment.

"She didn't do anything," Aurora said.

"Why are you crying again?" He didn't like her tears, they were the saddest thing he'd ever seen in his entire life. He wanted to kill something to make her feel better because that's what he knew he was capable of. Comfort, he didn't think he could do that.

"I was so afraid, Onyx."

"I know," he said softly, sitting by her bedside again and taking her hand.

"I wasn't just afraid of losing the baby, I was afraid of losing you."

"You barely tolerate me," he teased.

"I know it's stupid, but I want this baby with you and when I thought it was lost I was terrified that it would destroy the sort of peace we have made. I had started to imagine a life with you and the baby and how you'd teach it to do wolfy things and I really want that."

She wanted the baby with him. That wasn't the same thing as wanting him he realized, and his heart ached.

"Well, no worries. The baby is fine and here I am, ready to teach it *wolfy things*."

She nodded and dried her face. "Take me home?"

"I would love nothing more," he admitted but he knew they weren't talking about the same thing.

By the time they got home it was late and Onyx knew Aurora was exhausted, she kept almost falling asleep for the last half of the drive. But he also wasn't ready to just let her be alone.

"I'll make you tea and a little dinner," he said, not asking.

She didn't argue, just shuffled home and straight to the couch where she laid down. By the time he was bringing her a cup of tea she was asleep.

Onyx sat on the floor and studied her features. She was delicate in the face as well as body. He had been surprised when she revealed her stomach for the ultrasound. It was slightly rounded already. It was barely enough to notice, but of course he had memorized her body over the years, not because he wanted to, but because he couldn't help himself.

He heard her phone ring and grabbed it before it could wake her. He saw that it was the doctor's office and answered.

"Hello?"

"Can I speak with Ms. Port please."

"She's sleeping, but this is the father, can I take a message?"

"Mr. West?"

"Yes."

"We got back some of the bloodwork already and she's very low on iron, we are prescribing a supplement and she can pick that up at the pharmacy tomorrow."

"Thank you." Onyx hung up and turned to Aurora who was now awake and staring at him with a frown.

"Did you just answer my phone?"

"You were asleep, and it was the doctor's office."

She sat up fast, her eyes flashing with worry. "What's wrong?"

"You're low on iron so they are sending a prescription to the pharmacy, I'll pick it up tomorrow in town."

She nodded and picked up the tea he'd set on the table for her. "I shouldn't be surprised, I think that's a common issue with pregnancy."

"I'm making you a spinach salad," he proclaimed then headed to the kitchen. He wasn't taking no for an answer. When he heard the television click on he knew that she wasn't going to argue and his heart fluttered at her acceptance of his care. He took a quick detour and grabbed the blanket he knew she liked to cuddle on the couch with and brought it to her.

She blinked up at him with surprise and gave him the sweetest smile. "Thank you."

He couldn't speak as her brightness washed over him. She was pure sunshine and deserved everything good out of this life.

CHAPTER TWENTY-FOUR

Aurora didn't mind being taken care of. What she did mind was that Onyx refused to give her space. He'd stayed the night on the couch, *just in case*, and then made her a spinach and cheese omelet for breakfast and watched her eat every bite. The only reprieve she got was when he rushed to town for the prescription and more spinach.

"Do you think I'm Olive Oyl?" she asked with a laugh as he unloaded the groceries.

"Olive Oyl was Popeye's wife, not his mother," he replied, surprising her that he got the reference. "And yes, I want that baby strong and healthy."

"Even if it's a girl?"

"Of course," he scoffed and handed her the bottle of pills.

They went on like that for the next week. Onyx camped on her couch and cooked for her while she tried to enjoy summer before she'd be back at work. She had no more bleeding incidents, but she was very anxious to see Dr. Blithe again. Honestly she was hoping that the doctor would convince Onyx to relax.

"Do you want to take Peggy back to your house for the full moon or is she safest here?" she asked as they finished dinner.

"Are you going to let me sleep by your feet like last full moon?"

"It's not supposed to rain," she teased. "Don't you need to run and hunt? Piss on things?"

He gave her a look that said he didn't appreciate her minimizing his wolfish desires. "That doesn't take long and honestly I don't think I'll be going far, just like last time."

He looked away after saying it and started to do the dishes. She wanted to demand he tell her what he was hiding, but she didn't want to pry either. They'd had an amazing week together and she didn't want to mess that up. They still teased, well she teased him, but there wasn't the same malice behind it as before and he didn't reciprocate like he did before.

"How about you take Peggy home and lock her up. If you decide you've roamed enough and want to curl up on my floor for the night, just scratch at the back door."

"Sounds good."

After he left to do his full moon thing she called her mom to give an update on her life and then settled to watch a movie. It had barely started when there was a light scratch at the back door.

"Well, that didn't take long," she said with a smile. Halfway to the door she froze as she realized how excited she was to open it and see him, how much she anticipated his presence, and how much she'd become used to it. "Fuck, I think I like him," she whispered.

He scratched again and she let him in. He settled onto the floor in front of the couch and she patted his head absentmindedly as the movie played. But she couldn't really pay attention because she was trying to figure out when she'd fallen in serious like with her grumpy werewolf neighbor.

. . .

Onyx could tell something was bothering her, but more so than usual he couldn't ask her about it. At least in this form he had an excuse for his silence.

She was petting him like a dog and he always thought that would bother him, but it didn't. He loved the feel of her fingers in his fur. He wondered if she'd scratch his belly if he rolled over and the thought made him laugh in his head. She'd probably draw the line at that.

Usually she was asleep on the couch halfway through a movie but something was keeping her up tonight and it bothered him. He turned his head and licked her hand, whining up at her.

"Do you need to go to the bathroom?" she asked.

He growled then nuzzled her hand and got up. She followed but when he headed to her bedroom instead of the back door she stopped.

"What is this? Some kind of wolf trick to get me in bed?"

He huffed and walked to her, licked her hand, stuck his nose on her belly, then walked to the bedroom.

"You're pushy even as a wolf, Onyx." But she didn't argue, she just turned off the television and lights, locked the doors, and followed him to the bedroom. When she laid down he jumped up and curled at her feet. "Okay, but if I wake up and you're naked in my bed, that will probably be a violation of trust."

He huffed because he agreed but also, he didn't care. He was sleeping in her bed. He was getting his scent all over where she slept and his wolf was extremely satisfied with that.

Thankfully he woke early enough that although he was naked in her bed, she was still asleep and would never know it. He snuck out of her house and froze on her front porch.

They lived in the middle of nowhere, he never worried about being caught naked after a full moon. So of course today the delivery guy was parked with a package in hand as he snuck out of Aurora's house.

Onyx lifted a hand to the driver and strolled to his house as if it were no big deal. "She's asleep, don't ring the bell," he called over his shoulder. The whole town knew she was pregnant with his baby by now, so hearing he was sneaking naked out of her house wouldn't be all that surprising to them.

The man mumbled a wary agreement and continued up her walkway.

Onyx dressed then got to work finishing a small table. He looked at the rocking chair he'd finished a week before as he worked and wondered when it would be a good time to give it to Aurora. She hadn't been very firm in her answer of nursery plans when he brought it up. Her house wasn't large but it was big enough for two. He assumed she'd be making the office she used mostly to store her unused exercise equipment, into a nursery. The chair would go great in there by the window where it would get sun all day. He could picture her there, rocking the baby to sleep and it made his heart swell. He wanted to be a part of that magic but he was afraid to talk to her about it. The last week had been so nice and easy, they had really enjoyed each other's company. He didn't want to ruin that by forcing her to tell him what she saw as a future with him. He knew she was a little annoyed by his constant presence, but she was adjusting to it too. That didn't mean she was falling for him the same way he had for her.

Which is why he was still overwhelmed with protective instincts toward her, because there was so much uncertainty. It drove him and his wolf crazy. He decided today he'd make a little push. He would take the chair over this morning and bring up nursery plans again.

He worked until he saw her front door open and she walked out with mug in hand and picked up the package that had been left. She was dressed in her pajamas still, a pair of cotton shorts and matching tank. Her hair was up in a bun and she looked absolutely adorable. She looked his way and waved, he lifted a hand then turned away and wiped his hands off on a rag. As always he had sawdust all over his jeans and because it was already a hot morning he was wearing a flannel he'd ripped the sleeves off of at some point. He probably looked ridiculous but she'd seen him about the same every day so why did it matter now? He smoothed the hair that had fallen loose from his own bun then grabbed the chair and walked over to her house.

She was settled on her porch seat and watched him cross their yards and climb the steps with a curious look on her face.

He set the chair down in front of her. "I made this for you to rock the baby in."

"Onyx," she said with a gasp. "It's beautiful, too beautiful. Oh my god it must have taken you ages." She got up and touched it reverently.

He'd carved sunbursts into the back of the chair and although it had taken quite a while, he had loved every moment of its creation. "I'm glad you like it." His voice was rough with emotion.

"I can't accept this, you could sell it for a lot."

"I didn't make it to sell, I made it for you. You just have to decide where it should go. I think you should put it in the nursery, that is currently a storage room office," he said trying to lighten the mood.

Aurora shook her head, "Onyx—" she began but stopped when she met his gaze.

"I made it for you, I want you to use it to rock our baby by the window in that room, it gets great light all day."

Her eyes glistened with tears but he was pretty sure they were happy tears so he picked up the chair and took it inside. There wasn't much room in the office but he put it in there anyway, then he looked around with a frown.

"I know, I need to clean some of this out. I wish I had a garage like your place. I'd fill it with stuff I hate to get rid of," she laughed. "Maybe I should get one of those storage sheds."

"You can use my garage," he said quickly.

She rolled her eyes at him. "Right, and then where would you do your woodworking?"

He didn't have an answer. "Well, I could help you take out what you don't use, run it into town and donate it or whatever you want. If you really want a storage shed I'll pick one up and move it all out there."

She smiled at him and he felt like he'd won the lottery. "I'd appreciate the help and truthfully most of it needs to be donated. Claire would be very impressed if I started on this nursery before school begins again."

"Oh, Claire, I made her a table," he said awkwardly, rubbing at the back of his neck.

"Why would you make Claire a table? She electrocuted you."

"You poisoned me and I made you a chair," he pointed out.

"Well, I guess you have a point," she laughed.

They spent the rest of the day clearing out most of what was in the soon-to-be nursery. Onyx did all the heavy lifting and Aurora directed. He realized she had a very hard time letting things go and he liked knowing that about her, it felt personal and real.

"You have to let this go so you can make room for the baby in your life," he said when she debated over what she described as a *really great basket.*

"That's easy for you to say, you're not cleaning out a room of built up junk right now."

"I've done it before, I have an empty extra room at my house," he said. He hadn't meant to drop that bomb today, but here they were.

"No you don't. Did you forget I spent two days there making sure I hadn't murdered you?"

"The room that had boxes of hinges and odds and end wood pieces, I cleared it out the other day."

"Why?" she asked carefully.

He shrugged, "Just in case you and the baby wanted to have a space in my house."

"You mean the baby?"

"Sure, but you too. I mean, it just makes sense that you might want to nest at my house too."

Aurora crossed her arms over her chest and looked Onyx in the eyes. "What do you want?"

Panic filled him. "What do you mean?" he asked carefully.

"You and I were never friendly, it was fine, it worked. Now I'm pregnant with your baby and we've figured out a way to be friends. It is working, but you made a room in your house for *me* and the baby? You slept on my bed last night. You leave your cat here half the time, you even bought it an extra litter box to keep here, and I just don't understand what you're leading up to."

"This," he said simply, and closed the distance between them. He pulled her into his arms and pressed his lips to hers.

CHAPTER TWENTY-FIVE

Aurora didn't react at first, she was shocked by the action but the warmth and pressure of his lips against hers felt amazing. She melted on a groan, her body softening into his and if her arms hadn't been trapped between them she would have run them up into his hair and pulled it loose. She parted her lips, accepting him deeper and he groaned. His hands were on her lower back, holding her against him and she felt how hard he was for her. His tongue swept into her mouth gently, sharing his taste with her, it was musky and sweet. Everything about this moment felt soft and sweet and she wasn't sure if he was afraid of hurting her or if he was afraid of her rejecting him, but she knew he was holding back.

She didn't want him to hold back.

Aurora pulled away slightly and his hands dropped. The kiss stopped and he took a breath but she didn't let him get far. Her hands shot out to grab hold of his head and she pulled him back down, biting at his lower lip the way she wanted.

"Aurora," he groaned and his hands grasped her ass, forcing her hips to his as he ground against her, all gentleness gone. He took control of the kiss. His tongue invaded her mouth and his teeth nipped at her until she felt devoured and she was left panting.

"Onyx," she gasped as his mouth moved to her neck.

The word spurred him on and he lifted her until she wrapped her legs around his waist and then he was moving, taking them to her bedroom. She worked quickly to release his hair from its tie as he walked, wanting to giggle with delight when it fell free and tickled against her skin. It carried with it the scent of his shampoo, something light and lavender. It surprised her, she would have pictured him showering with some scent called *Bear Spit*, or something else as manly.

"Tell me you want this," Onyx said against her neck.

"I definitely want this." She wasn't sure what it would mean for them, or what would happen next, but in that moment she knew she didn't want him to stop. "Condoms are in the drawer by the bed."

He laid her on the bed then leaned over her with a grin. "I think it's too late to worry about pregnancy."

"Funny. I just, you know, safety first," she said with an awkward shrug. This wasn't the best time to bring up the fact that he likely slept with strangers at the bar, but she wasn't stupid, she knew what was out there.

"I will wear one if you want but just so you know, I haven't been with anyone in a long time, and I'm clean."

"You were at the bar like a month ago," she pointed out.

Onyx stood up and pulled his shirt over his head. She eyed his tattoos hungrily, she'd always wanted to run her tongue across them.

"Just because I went for a drink, doesn't mean I slept with someone," he pointed out, bringing her attention back to what they had been discussing.

"Oh." She felt stupid for assuming he was like every other guy she'd ever known, he was nothing like anyone she'd ever met. "Okay, I'm clean too."

His hands stilled on his pants. "Aurora, I feel like I just pressured you."

She sat up. "No Onyx, I am not a pushover, now take your pants off."

He growled but obeyed. His pants came off and he pushed her back with his mouth on her breasts, which thanks to pregnancy, were spilling over the top of her bra. She had never been a very busty woman and it hadn't bothered her, but she had caught Onyx looking at her growing chest a few times over the last month and she had to admit she liked the way they attracted his attention.

As his tongue followed the line of her top she arched up and his hands slipped down to pull up the hem. He sat back on the bed as he slowly pulled the shirt up, revealing her to him. His eyes watched reverently as her pert nipples popped free. He threw his head back and howled.

The sound surprised her so much she laughed and when he looked back at her with a sheepish grin she reached up to put her palms on his face. "Onyx, are you going to go wolfy? Because I think that's something I need to be warned about beforehand."

"No, just couldn't hold back the excitement," he admitted. "I don't think you understand how much I am enjoying this."

She trailed her hands down his chest to the bulge in his boxers. "I think I have an idea."

He groaned at her touch then leaned down to lick her nipples. It wasn't long before she was squirming with need and he kissed his way down to her stomach. She loved the way his hair felt against her skin and she couldn't resist running her fingers through it as he moved lower.

He paused just below her belly button, his nose pressed to her skin and he inhaled deeply. He kissed her sweetly there then moved lower. She was wearing elastic pajama shorts which she was thankful for as he quickly pulled them and her underwear off. Then he was sitting up and staring at her again, now fully nude. She'd never been self-conscious in situations like this but the way his eyes seemed to be trying to memorize every inch of her body had her feeling like a work of art.

"Aurora, you're more beautiful than I could have ever imagined." He trailed a finger from her thigh up between her breasts. Then his gaze met hers and he smiled. His smile was transformative on his usually gruff face. She never wanted it to leave. She thought in that moment she'd do anything to keep him smiling at her like that forever.

He leaned over her, kissing her again with sweet softness as he removed his boxers then he laid his body on hers, skin to skin, as his tongue made slow sweeps through her mouth. His hands worked to let her hair loose and then sat back to spread it out around her. "Beautiful," he whispered then he was kissing her again. His movements drove her desire high and she rubbed against him, wanting and ready. But he was in no hurry and moved his mouth to her neck again then nipped at her ear.

"Impatient," he chastised when her hands gripped his ass and she widened her legs in encouragement.

"I know what I want," she countered.

"Do you?" he challenged and slid his hands down her sides leaving a trail of heat as he briefly gripped her hips, pushing them down. Then his hands moved up to cup her sensitive breasts. His fingers flicked across her nipples and he watched her face. She didn't even try to hide how much she was enjoying his touch. She gasped and arched and ran her hands up and down his back. "When I take you, I am going to lose my fucking mind. So I want you to be out of your mind with desire before that happens."

"Fuck," she groaned, his words sending a new spike of desire straight to her clenching pussy. She knew she was wet and ready, but she couldn't deny that his worshipful technique was taking her to a level she'd never reached.

One of his hands moved up to cup her chin as his mouth descended to hers and his other snaked down between them, and finally he was touching her where she needed it most. She ran her hands up and down his back, scoring lightly with her nails and making him shiver. She opened her mouth on a gasp as his finger skated across her clit and he kissed her deep and hard. His fingers found her wet opening and when he pushed in she broke the kiss to scream, it felt so good. "Oh fuck, Onyx."

"Yes, that's next," he whispered and nipped at her ear. "First, come on my fingers, sunshine, I need to feel it."

She clung to him, her body all too eager to do exactly what he asked. He bit lightly on her shoulder and neck as his fingers pumped in and out slowly, but she needed more. She let out a whine and tried to move her hips but his body was keeping her down.

"Onyx, I need more, I can't—" she stopped as he added another finger and his thumb skated over her clit. His other hand moved to her neck, holding her steady with just a little pressure and that was it, she came. Her body convulsed under him and she didn't hold back her screams of pleasure as he continued his movements in and out of her. His mouth was hot and sharp on her shoulder and she didn't care if he left a mark there for all to see, she was sure he'd just written his name on her soul.

Onyx was about to lose himself, but he'd known that he needed her ready for him. He wasn't sure if she knew what was about to happen, but he could feel it.

Just as her convulsions around his fingers started to slow, he moved into position. With one hand on her leg he lifted it up and away while the other hand went to his cock. He leaned up to see her face as he slammed into her. The first pump was heaven and he thought he'd like to die just then because nothing in his life would ever compare, he was sure, so why even try. But then he pulled out and pushed in again and it was just as amazing.

Her deep green eyes were on him, still hazy with desire. "Fuck, you feel so good I'm not going to hold back."

"Don't hold back."

"I can feel it coming."

"Okay, that's fine, I already came," she said encouragingly.

"No, my knot, I'm going to knot you and—" just saying it was more than he could take. He slammed into her one more time and the knot at the base of his cock swelled inside her, locking him in place. She screamed as it rubbed against her g-spot and although his movements were nearly halted, he grabbed her hips and began to move her, rubbing her over his knot as she panted toward another orgasm.

"Onyx, I didn't, oh fuck, Onyx," she screamed as she came again setting off his own intense orgasm. His vision went dark as his body spasmed and then he collapsed. He grabbed her and spun them so she was on top and not suffocating under his temporarily incapacitated body.

They didn't move for a few minutes. Sweaty and breathing heavy, they clung to each other. Their hair was a mingled mess and it clung to their bodies. He liked the sight and ran his hands over the light and dark locks.

"Why didn't you tell me?" she asked after a while.

"I didn't know it was going to happen until we'd already started," he said, guessing she was referencing his knot.

"It was ... is fine, um, how long before it lets me go?"

Onyx stiffened with mortification. "I don't know."

"You've never uh, knotted before?"

"It only happens sometimes, usually your first time. It should go down soon." He couldn't tell her the truth, that it only happened the first time and then when you found someone who your wolf thought was a perfect mate.

"Oh, okay, well this is slightly awkward."

"Why?"

"Because don't you want to get up?"

"Why? Do you want me to get up?"

"It's just that usually a guy is up after, you know," she shrugged.

He didn't like what she was saying. It sounded like everyone else she'd slept with had been an asshole who couldn't wait to move on with his day after getting what he wanted. It made him want to find them all and shove his fist in their faces. Then again, he kind of liked that he was giving her more things that no one else had.

"Aurora, I want to be right here with you. Do you want me to get up and leave?"

"No, not at all," she assured him and her hands swept up and down his arms. "This is nice."

He grabbed her face gently and lifted it so he could kiss the freckles on her nose. "Yes it is," he agreed and buried his nose in her neck. You smell amazing, did you know that?"

"Like sweat and sex?" she asked with a giggle.

"Yes." He wanted to live in this scent, it would tell everyone they passed that they belonged to each other.

"That's a wolf thing, right? You can smell so much more?"

He laughed. "Yeah, it's a wolf thing."

"Okay. Will you be offended if I shower?"

"Not at all, it will just mean I have to mark you again."

"*Mark* me?"

Shit, he felt a trap underfoot. "I just mean that this was enjoyable, and I'd like to do it again."

She leaned up and raised an eyebrow. "No you don't, you want to mark me so everyone stays away, don't you?"

"Would it be so wrong if I did?" he asked, his finger tracing the slight bite mark he'd left on her shoulder.

"I honestly don't know, Onyx. Things between us are complicated."

"Things between us are linked." He gestured to her stomach

and further down where their bodies were literally stuck together.

"How much would it hurt if I jumped off of you right now?" she asked with a frown.

He grabbed her hips in a firm grip. "A lot," he snarled.

"So I have you at my mercy?" She leaned forward and put her elbows on his chest and her chin on her hands. Her lips curved up in a mischievous smile.

"You do," *more than you could ever imagine.*

"So tell me, Onyx, was this your plan? You've been hanging around, pissing on my lawn and making me dinner. Did you just want to sleep with me?"

"Yes, I definitely wanted to sleep with you for a while now but no, that wasn't what I was doing all that for."

"Then what? Real talk. What is happening here?"

Onyx let out a sigh and felt his knot deflate. She must have as well because she sat up and slid off of him. He wanted to tell her to come back but just watched as she got off the bed and grabbed a robe. When she was covered, she turned to him and the vulnerable look on her face made his heart ache.

Onyx sat up and nodded. "Real talk. I want you and the baby and everything that entails. I want your sunshine in my life and I want to sleep with you every night. I want it so bad it scares me because it's everything I thought I never wanted. My knot only comes out for my mate and you're it, you are my mate. If you don't want me then I will still be a father to the baby because that matters to me too, but that's not what this is about. I know you think it is, or worry that it is all about the baby and somehow when it comes out I won't want you anymore but that's not true. Aurora, you are the sunshine my life has been missing, the heat and heart I didn't even know I needed until I let down a few walls and started to feel you."

"Onyx," she said with a hiccup and a tear fell down her face.

Onyx braced himself for rejection but she threw herself at him and kissed him passionately.

"Onyx, I want you too. You are grumpy and ridiculous and I want to be your bit of sunshine. I want to see what we can do together, you and me and this little bean."

Onyx placed both hands on her stomach and felt his life settle. "We'll do this thing."

"I just have one very important question."

"Uh oh."

"Do you knot every time we have sex?"

"I'm afraid so."

"So I guess that means no anal?"

His head snapped up and his mouth dropped open as he met her eyes but the mischievous look there told him she was joking. "Oh, you think so do you?" he growled and spun so he was hovering over her again, her loosely tied robe fell open to reveal her perfect body and he was hard again, ready to take her any way she wanted him.

CHAPTER TWENTY-SIX

When Aurora stepped out of the shower she stood in front of the mirror and examined her body. There were a few love marks here and there and she smiled as she touched each one, remembering how Onyx had given them to her. She'd given him a few too, when she'd finally gotten to kiss and nip along his tattoos. And now he was in her kitchen making dinner. She couldn't believe they were really going to try and do this together thing. She wanted to call Claire and spill everything but she couldn't while he was in the house, his hearing was way too good.

Then she remembered he'd said he had a table for Claire and her heart swelled all over again. He hated everyone yet he'd made her best friend a table so she wouldn't have to buy a cheap one. He was a good guy. He just didn't give his goodness out to everyone and there was nothing wrong with that. It made it even more special to know he was giving it to her now.

"Oh my god you fucked him," Claire said as Onyx hauled her new table out of the back of his truck.

"Shh, he has like supernatural hearing."

"Well I assume he also knows you fucked him," Claire laughed.

"Yes," Aurora whisper hissed. "We're kind of together. Did you know that they knot when they are with someone they really like."

"Like? You mean mate. He mated you, you're werewolf married," Claire said, eyes wide.

Aurora groaned because her friend refused to be serious and it was her favorite thing about her, but today she wasn't sure she could handle it. "I don't think that's how it works."

"I am," she said with a grin and pulled Aurora in for a side hug. "Congratulations."

"I'll be needing a second opinion."

"You could always have your dad ask his partner."

"Gross!"

"What's gross?" Onyx asked from the porch.

"Werewolves," Claire said with a grin. "But she must have a stronger stomach than me."

Onyx bared his teeth at her but didn't growl, which Aurora thought was an improvement.

"Want to stay for lunch? I have a new table to use," Claire asked.

"No, we have to get to a doctor's appointment, but maybe tomorrow?"

"Definitely," she agreed. They hugged and then Aurora got in Onyx's truck and they were on their way.

"You told her," he accused.

"She guessed."

That put a wide grin on his face. "I guess I marked you well even though you showered off my scent."

Aurora smacked his arm playfully, but it was true there was a visible hickey on her neck. It was way too hot to wear clothes that would cover it.

"I don't care who knows," he said after a minute.

"But what exactly do we tell them? I'm not really interested in going around and saying I fucked my neighbor. But we haven't been together long enough to announce a relationship."

"I've known you for three years, that's a long time," Onyx argued.

"But you hated me for most of it."

"Hate is a strong word," he grumbled.

They let the subject drop until they were once again sitting in Shayla's exam room. When she walked in she took one look at them and huffed. "So I guess you two are together now?"

"Yes," Onyx said for both of them and Aurora didn't bother correcting the doctor, what did it matter anyway. They were trying this thing, people could assume whatever about what that meant.

Shayla went through her list of questions and looked at Aurora's chart then pulled out the ultrasound machine. "We are going to take a look just to make sure the placenta is okay after the bit of a scare you had."

"Okay," Aurora said but she felt like a brick had landed on her chest. The doctor was worried enough to want to look, that wasn't good.

Onyx grabbed her hand as Shayla arranged the machine and Aurora's clothes. She squirted on the warm goop then the wand swooped around her belly. An image appeared quickly on the screen this time.

"It looks like a gerbil," Onyx said but his voice was soft and he had an adoring look on his face.

"They all look like that at this stage, don't worry," Shayla said, a hint of amusement in her voice. "You won't be giving birth to a puppy."

Aurora snorted. "Is there any way to tell if it'll have more werewolf features or human?" Aurora asked.

"No, unfortunately you might not know fully until puberty. If the child develops shifting abilities or not won't be known before that. You might notice some things like heightened senses or eating habits earlier."

"But it will be fine?" she prodded. She needed the reassurance, probably would every time she came in until she gave birth and could look at her perfect little baby every day to reassure herself.

"It will be perfect," Shayla said and then pulled off the wand and wiped the gel from Aurora's belly. "The placenta looks good too but let me know immediately if you have any more bleeding or any pain."

"I will," Onyx said quickly and Aurora met Shayla's eyes with a look that indicated they both thought he was stupid for answering *that* question.

As they were about to leave the clinic Aurora told Onyx she'd forgotten her purse in the room and hurried back.

Shayla sat in the room with Aurora's purse on her lap. "Purse?" Shayla said with a knowing look. "No woman leaves her purse. What did you need to talk to me about?"

Aurora was glad she wasn't going to have to go search for her in the clinic. "I want to know what it means when a werewolf knots during sex and I need to know if I'm werewolf married," she said, feeling like an idiot even as the words spilled out of her.

Shayla looked surprised but she didn't look like Aurora's questions were unhinged. "He knotted?"

Aurora nodded.

"It means his wolf picked you."

That's basically what Onyx had told her but she felt like he'd held something back.

"It also means that you'll never be able to get rid of him. If you break up he'll follow you like a puppy because he loves you." She shrugged like it was no big deal.

Meanwhile Aurora's head was spinning at the L word.

"There's no such thing as werewolf married, it's called mated and yeah, he mated you. If you were a werewolf you would feel that too but you're human so it's different, your emotions are more confusing."

"Yeah they are," she sighed. "Especially now."

"Can I give you some advice?"

"I think that's why I'm here."

"If you're not interested in being his mate, cut off everything now. Stringing him along will turn him feral and I have a feeling he was halfway there already."

No pressure, Aurora thought as she left the room clutching her purse. When she saw Onyx waiting for her with an anxious set to his features that melted with relief when his gaze landed on her, her heart stuttered.

She didn't want to cut anything off with him she realized. She hurried across the waiting room and pulled him down for a kiss.

"Well hello," he said when she pulled away.

"I think I'm falling in love with you," she admitted.

"Did you take drugs while you were back there?" he asked.

Aurora smacked his chest playfully. "Is that seriously your response?"

He pulled her close and buried his face in her neck then laid a soft kiss just below her ear. "I know I am falling in love with you and those words made my cock swell so if you don't want me to drag you to the bathroom, let's save the rest of this conversation for later."

Aurora giggled and let him lead her out of the building.

They didn't make it farther than his truck. Onyx pulled her into the backseat and shoved her shorts and underwear off while kissing her. Her body heated and she ran her hands over his back and chest, wanting to touch his skin but knowing this wasn't one of those sorts of times. This was sex in a car, fast and furious.

Onyx pushed his own pants down as he shoved his fingers into her. She gasped and he groaned. "Fuck, you're ready for me."

"Yes," she agreed and lifted her hips.

He pushed his thick cock into her and she savored the feeling.

Her eyes closed and she bit her lip to keep quiet. His hands gripped her hips as he set a frantic pace that drove her quickly toward orgasm. His thumb moved to flick across her clit and she fisted his hair, thankful he'd left it loose today, as the pressure built. She was going to come.

"Onyx, oh god, I'm so close," she gasped in his ear.

"Me too, I can't—" he slid out of her suddenly and shifted her body so fast she couldn't understand what was happening. Her legs went over his shoulders and his mouth was on her clit as he groaned and she felt the wet spurts of him coming against her back.

She covered her mouth with an arm as she cried out with the orgasm his tongue expertly dragged from her. She hoped they didn't get the cops called on them, this was definitely indecent exposure. He licked and sucked as her body convulsed. He didn't stop until she did and then he set her down gently. She realized he was kneeling on the seat facing her.

"Why did you do that?" she asked, not that she minded, it was amazing.

"Didn't want to get stuck together back here, it's not the most comfortable spot for knotted cuddling," he admitted with a grin.

Aurora sat up and moved so she could investigate the knot. His cock had softened some but the baseball size knot around the base was engorged and red. She licked her lips thinking about how she really wanted to touch it and explore it, but she didn't know if he'd like that.

"It's okay, it's not painful," he said, misinterpreting her gaze.

"Can I touch it?" she asked.

He groaned and nodded eagerly.

She reached out a hand and stroked a finger around the knot.

Onyx gasped and a fresh spurt of come dribbled out the tip of his cock. She reached her hand around the knot and squeezed gently and Onyx lifted his hips. "Aurora we should go before we get caught."

"I think not," she said and gave it another gentle squeeze, then leaned forward and took the tip of his cock in her mouth.

"Shit," he growled and his hands gripped her ponytail, holding her there while his hips moved and she felt herself getting wet again as he spurted into her mouth and she massaged his knot. She pushed her free hand between her wet thighs and fingered her clit, needing to release again as she dragged the last bits of his release from his knot.

Onyx growled a deep rumbling sound and his knot finally deflated with a final burst of his come on her tongue. It sent her over the edge and she jolted with an orgasm as he dragged her up and slammed his lips to hers.

"You are fucking perfection, sunshine, did you know that? I am not sure that I deserve you, but I will die trying to."

"You deserve me," she whispered against his lips.

CHAPTER TWENTY-SEVEN

Aurora felt like a blimp. It was spring break and the weather was cool but she couldn't really enjoy it because she was enormous and due any day now. No matter how many times Onyx told her she was beautiful, she found it hard to believe most days when nothing fit and she wanted to cry.

"Hey, do you want to take a drive? We can go to the ocean, maybe stop and see your dad after?" Onyx asked as he rubbed her feet. They were in his house, which was kind of theirs now since she was half moved in. They were taking it a little slow and there were definitely no marriage plans. She refused to even talk about it until she felt like her body belonged to herself again and Onyx agreed to wait until after the birth. She had a feeling he wasn't going to wait much longer than that, and honestly she was okay with it. She knew they were it for each other.

"I think that would be a good distraction."

He gave her a tight smile and she wondered what was going on, but she'd learned that he would tell her when he was ready. She started to feel uncomfortable about halfway there but didn't want to make a big deal about it. She figured it was probably indigestion or Braxton Hicks, nothing to worry about, and if she told Onyx then he would worry, a lot. He'd already rushed her to the birthing center twice in the last month for nothing. She didn't need that embarrassment again.

They drove to the coast and he turned the truck south. She could tell he had a destination in mind but she didn't know what it was and couldn't concentrate on asking as she wiggled through another pain.

Onyx took roads as familiar to him as his own hand but also different than he remembered because twenty years changed a lot. He stopped the truck at the end of a gated road. Just outside of the gate was the broken-down remnants of a house and beyond the trees he could just make out the roof of another he had no doubt was in great condition.

Aurora's soft touch on his arm made him jump. "Is this your family's land?" she asked.

"I'm not really sure if it still is. My father died a few years back. I only know that because a lawyer showed up on my doorstep. My father left me a little money which was a shock, I don't know who got the house."

"You have four living siblings, right?"

"I believe I do. The oldest is Jeanie and despite her being a girl I bet my dad left her his business. She was smart as fuck, probably even smarter than Tanner had been, definitely smarter than me."

"You're too hard on yourself Onyx. Just because you didn't want to follow in your father's footsteps doesn't mean you aren't smart, maybe it means you're too smart."

He smiled at her because he wanted to believe her.

"Do you want to knock?"

"No, I don't want to disturb anyone, I just wanted to see it. I was so angry when I left here, so determined that I wouldn't ever let my life be controlled by my father or anyone else."

Aurora made a little distressed noise and her hand left his arm to rub her belly.

"No," he said quickly. "No I don't see this baby as control, Aurora. I see it as the first thing in twenty years that has felt like pack."

"I know, and you don't have to exclude them from our life."

The way she said *our life* made his heart swell. "I know, but I don't even know them anymore and I think that's okay." He started the truck and drove away. When he looked in the rearview mirror he saw a young woman standing by the gate with the look of Tanner mixed with Rebecca. Everyone here had lived their life while he was gone and so had he. But now his life was changing again and as he drove away from his family's home this time, he felt no hatred for them. He felt calm in his understanding that they weren't part of his future, they weren't what the goddess intended for him and no one could fight Her will.

"I know I say this all the time, Aurora, but I'm so happy to be having a baby with you."

"Today?" she asked.

Onyx laughed. "You know what I mean."

"No, Onyx. Today," she said and groaned.

He shot his gaze to her and pushed on the gas. "You're in labor?"

"I think so. I thought it was like the other times and it would stop but it's not stopping, it's getting worse."

"Aurora," he growled. How had she kept this from him? But he knew how. He'd been super distracted by this little trip and she didn't want him to freak out like before about a little pain so she'd been trying to hide it. "We are not going to make it to the birthing center are we?"

"There's one in Oceanview, take me there. The clinic has the same doctors on rotation there, it'll be someone we know."

He got her there but then panicked because they didn't have their bag, he wasn't prepared.

She just smiled at him. "Hey, calm down, it's fine. Claire will get the bag and bring it here. I already texted her."

"But your pillow and blanket. I want the baby to smell us when it comes out, not hospital."

"Are you planning to be in the room?"

"Of course."

"Then it'll smell us."

He nodded frantically and helped her into the birthing center.

Three hours later Dr. Shayla was handing Aurora a baby girl. "Congratulations mom and dad," she said.

Aurora burst into tears as the squirming gooey girl was placed on her chest and Onyx kissed her forehead.

"You gave me a little girl," he whispered. "I hope she's just like you."

"Is there a name for her?" Shayla asked.

"Sunny Beatrice West," Aurora said, smiling up at Onyx. They'd already discussed names for both genders but she'd had a feeling it would be a girl to carry on her family's tradition.

"I like it, sort of old fashioned," Shayla said.

"It's strong, like the women she comes from," Onyx said, smoothing the hair back from Aurora's forehead.

"She's got a pretty tough father's side as well and if I were to judge by those big feet and ears, she's going to have some shifter abilities."

Aurora touched her daughter's feet and smiled at Onyx. "I hope so. Her daddy will love to teach her all about running through the forest and catching rabbits."

"I can't wait," Onyx agreed. "Marry me?"

"Okay," she said and kissed him. "But you know it isn't fair to ask me questions while I'm high on birth."

"Yeah but I figured it was my best chance. Got to lock you down before you start thinking reasonably again."

He kissed her and slipped a ring on her finger.

"You had that on you just in case but not the birthing bag?"

"I've been carrying it around every day for six months," he admitted.

Aurora couldn't love him more. She pulled him down for a kiss over their daughter.

Felicity Stonecroft had never encountered this before but she knew the Moon Goddess was behind it. She felt Her tendrils of manipulation all over it. What she didn't understand was why the goddess was concerning herself with the affairs of a demon.

"Do we have an understanding?" the demon asked as he took the cup from her.

"You know I am a willing conduit of the goddess's mischief."

"So I've been told," he said darkly and walked into one of the specimen deposit rooms.

Felicity felt the sparks of the goddess as she walked to the room where her next client was waiting for insemination. "I'm sorry, it'll just be a few minutes. I'm waiting for the sample, it's being prepared right now."

MEET THE AUTHOR

Courtney Davis is an author of romance across many genres including paranormal, space, and fantasy. She lives with her family in North Idaho where she enjoys reading and writing when she isn't teaching or soaking up the sunshine. She strives to create worlds full of diverse characters and romance that intrigues readers.

OTHER TITLES FROM

5 PRINCE PUBLISHING